# THE Dream of the Black Topaze Chamber

I0666192

## HUGH FOX

SKYLIGHT PRESS

First published in Great Britain in 2011 by Skylight Press,
210 Brooklyn Road, Cheltenham, Glos GL51 8EA

The Poem Cycle for *The Dream of the Black Topaze Chamber* was published in
chapbook form in 1983 by Ghost Pony Press, Wisconsin, USA.

Cover painting by Mikki Nylund: "And Her Mirror", Mixed Media on Canvas,
2011. www.mikkinylund.com

Designed and typeset by Rebsie Fairholm
Publisher: Daniel Staniforth

Printed and bound in Great Britain by Lightning Source, Milton Keynes

www.skylightpress.co.uk

ISBN 978-1-908011-39-8

# THE DREAM OF THE BLACK TOPAZE CHAMBER

**i.**

As hard as she tried, Magda couldn't remember her first meeting with Bernadette.

"But you shook hands, talked … " Bernadette insisted.

It had been after Nona's lecture on "The University as Anti-Think" (as in Anti-Christ), and Magda could kind of remember, but not really-really, Bernadette remaining for her a vague shadow of a figure lost in an audience, small, like The Dead trying to break through into the Now, wanting to come back and not making it. But the second meeting was very vivid, in front of Riachuelo Supermercado, Bernadette 31, fading flower, African violets, lilacs, those were to become her colours. Well, they already were, her closet was full of Violet Day and shimmering Black Night, but at that Riachuelo meeting-point on her time-track, she was still all clinical white most of the time.

"Well, it's the pressure of the profession," she complains, when Magda tells her how she remembers her, "one of the whys of getting out, mainly because it is mute and invisible … "

And everything she did at that time was in the context of her father's influence too.

"My mother had just died six months before (the photos of her mother just like her, the same thin face, she even insists that 'As you get older your nose lengthens, at least mine will … I'll become the thin, sad, sagging old lady in the picture on the dining room wall') and my father … it seems so 'small' on my part to dehumanize him to the sound of slippers shuffling along the tiled floors, but that's practically all he is for me. I might even say was, always has been … although sometimes when we were kids he broke down and played, even got down on the floor and played Horse, and we'd even ride him, the whole room would turn into a circus, and all nine of us would be so happy … it's never the money or the lack of it, we really are first spirit and the body comes trailing after, the whole house would become a big Festa … and then all, of a sudden, click, it'd all turn off, he'd inexplicably get angry, tired of it all, and he'd close it all down, we'd descend to earth again. He'd sit at one end of the tea-time table and I'd sit at the other, and the whole universe was between us. It was unthinkable to try to reach across through all that space, all that hiss of emptiness … "

Back in front of Riachuelo. Nona's the 'contact,' Bernadette's with her in Advanced Conversation (English) down at Fiske and she and Nona come out each with a bag of groceries in their arms, and Bernadette comes out, a tiny little bag held in her fingers.

"It's Bettina's birthday, I just came to get some things to decorate the cake with. I'd drive you home, but ..."

"I wouldn't think of it," says Nona.

"A plastic surgeon," says Magda, thinking of her, really, as 'rooty'-looking, runty, never anticipating the worlds in her closet that were just waiting to be activated, "how about doing a job on me ... " jaw, eyes, beginning to look full-time like The Volga Boatwoman.

"OK," she says, smiling her fading violet smile, thinking Magda was kidding, as she told her later, "I thought you were kidding. Any time anyone meets me they almost always say something about surgery. Especially the stomach. Everyone wants pizza and cookies and tiny little bellies, damn the blood and stitches ... "

Vera Sabina. Later on they'll go out to her place in the interior of the island, wide, windy loghouse on a hill in front of the cupped hand curve of an abandoned quarry, and they'll see EARLY SABINA, with a volume of Picasso's etchings on the corner of her work-table. Magda wanted to buy one strong, Picassoesque drawing of tree-women/women-trees, breasts and vaginas, especially breasts torturously emerging out of tree-forms, Magda thinking, when she saw LATE(R) SABINA, over at Carmen's house, or like here in Bernadette's office, all over the walls, wormform-faces sculpted into blue-purple-red jungle, that the earliest was the best and strongest, although the late(r) was the smoothest, more ovarian-uterine, Self entregandose/surrendering itself to the soft purple fingers of massage-night ... The whole room hummed in the rich iris-tones on the unconscious side of the spectrum.

"I wasn't kidding when I said I wanted surgery," says Magda.

Bernadette fingering her eyes, temples, pulling up, moulding the Slavic slips and sags of flesh.

"You have such a pretty face now," says Bernadette, "you don't really need surgery ... "

"I hate the upper lids," says Magda, "this overhang of flesh, Czechoslovakia genetically asserting itself against my will. And the neck, bull-neck ... I hate it. Every year I hate it more. I'm becoming my peasant grandmother. When I was twenty I thought I'd escaped, now that I'm almost fifty I feel pulled down into the Slavic whirlpool of racial melancholia ... "

"I never would have thought you're fifty," says Bernadette.

She's "soft" here in her blue-violet world, and in the middle of the maintained distance, what is Magda feeling? Night between her legs ...

"What I'd like ... do you give private English classes?"

4

"I do."

"I'm thinking of going to Canada. Physical therapy. My brother's going to Waterloo for his Ph.D. in Electrical Engineering."

"And my surgery?"

"Let me think about it … Deixa-me pensar … "

Which is what Magda always says in stores when she knows she's not coming back.

That night Nona complaining.

"That's customer-robbing, isn't it? She was my student first."

"She wants private lessons, maybe she doesn't like groups."

A little electric heater on, in the middle of their second cold June, in Magda's (the big) room under this purple, pineapple-shaped (if you study it carefully) light, the kids asleep in the room which is where Nona sleeps too, always with them, the abiding Mother Presence. It's interesting to see how stable they are, the "foreign" country, Brazil, not "foreign" at all for them, fitting in from almost the first day, nervous systems that always say HOME where- and when-ever … as long as they're together. It's a thing Nona and Magda talk a lot about, PRESENCE, in the violet-uterine light, all wrapped in/poured into binding black ballet nylon, their legs touching, Magda at the head, Nona at the foot of the bed, Nona knitting (already – seven months away) sweaters for her Kansas City nieces, Magda with a copy of Celso Furtado's *Formação Econômica do Brasil* grudgingly on the bed in front of her.

"Well, she doesn't talk in class at all … I mean at all," says Nona.

"Something about wanting to go to Canada."

"I don't know, she's very private, she's one of those people you never really *know*-know … "

"Maybe," says Magda.

Chapter 34, *Readjustamento do Coeficiente de Importações* … Readjustment of the Coefficient of Imports.


**ii.**

They pick up the kids at Coração de Jesús, the two women, everyone wondering about them … are they widows or divorced, or … ?

It's all hens, a hen-courtyard. Tia (teacher)-hens, nun-hens, Mother-of-God hens, Mediterranean Virgin-Hen courtyard, cold and windy in the Santa Catarina winter afternoon. You look up and it's Illinois-Michigan January, thin ascetic cirrus bone-flake clouds, then your eye travels back to Earth across palms. But you're still cloaked with cold. Taxi home, short way via Saco dos Limões, along the Beira Mar water-front, vertiginously heady sea-winds and waves, then up into the green hills (Pantanal), up their private driveway, through the iron gates. Home.

Pica-Pau Amarelo's on the TV, a corn-doll becomes "real" (Visconde) and a second (younger) corn-doll also becomes "real," and there's all this business about the two dolls being two stages of the same "being" ... and the talking breadfruit tree.

The trouble is that you look out off the back verandah at the purple-flowered vines and humming birds and moths sucking the flowers and another moth flies by with a peacock eye on the outer brown side of the wing, an iridescent blue underside, and there's the spiders and a snake slithering across the grass, there's the samurai rustling of the bamboo, and "reality" becomes more fantastic than TV "fantasy."

Magda comes inside, Nona's getting dinner ready. Walks into her room, Puta-Night between her thighs, black, membranously-webbed legs and nippleless webbed bra (food is the enemy, the over-abundance of Middle-Class Middle-Age), black suede boots and lace skirt and top, the mouth between her legs, her other belly empty/hungry. She fluffs out her blonde curly hair. With all her sagging, squaring jowls, if it wasn't for Brazil with always something on the TV about renovation, perpetual hope, renewal, the Land of Never-Die, she would have just given up.

Magda squeezes her legs together.

What's Nona making? Hamburgers? Well ... the kids ...

Eyeliner, mascara, this almost-black lipstick, then out into the kitchen, French Fries and hamburgers.

"Hi ... " says Magda.

"Hi ... "

"Can I help you?"

"I don't know, we need something to drink. Maybe you could make some orange juice ... "

"And ... ?"

Nona turning around. She's got on these transparent plastic shoes with black roses on the vamp.

"Great, you look great ... " she says, giving Magda the once-over.

And Magda, instead of feeling "up," feels "down" all of a sudden. It's skillets and grease, dead meat and Cabocla on the TV now. It's one show she can't seem to get into, although the kids like it, the authenticity, the (young) female they can always identify with. Dark out now. Magda's dark-red fingernail polish almost black, cutting and juicing oranges, thinking ADD A TOUCH OF CANELA (vanilla) TO THE JUICE, but doesn't, no-one'll drink it then, setting out plates and silverware, everything ready. She grabs Nona. Nona responds, but ...

"What's wrong?"

"Why now?"

"Why not? Really, what's wrong?"

"That hair. And then the eyes and the black lace. It's Wednesday, you've got a seven-thirty class in the morning ... "

"So? OK ... "

Magda feels like taking off all the sex-clothes and make-up, letting her hair go grey, becoming just as dowdy as she really is under all the theatrics, 47, 48 ...

"Later, OK?" says Nona, "I love you ... "

This horse-/dog-patting, nudging. Magda sits down at the table, calls the girls, "Alexandra, Margaret," they don't budge, "when this programme's over ... " she goes in and talks to them, comes back in, coffee and orange-juice, Magda nibbles a couple of french fries.

"Come on," says Nona, "we'll get together later ... "

"I'm OK."

Later under covers, in the cold, Nona naked and Magda in elastic black, Nona can't resist Magda the Whore, although, even as gay as she is, she never really sheds her "straightness," the ancestral line of Methodist prairie sanity, the wilderness ploughed and tamed, her (Nona's) grandmother's voice eternal there in the sane (pioneer) dark, "We'd get one orange a year ... at Christmas ... " sagebrush rolling across the bed and through the jungle green turned dustbowl.


### iii.

September, Magda on the verandah, second floor back, on a blanket all wrapped against the cold, wearing her heaviest tights, writing:

... flesh-sand crumbling
under night-hand
clamped around bone-flesh
meshed in powdered-jasmine
time, the disguise off ...


Stops,

the green catface of the jungle all around her, how high the bamboo grows before it (Chartres-Gothic) arches down, and the eucalyptus in bloom, the air and the verandah-deck filled with the scuds of blossoms. Wild bananas, two bunches almost ready to be picked, and trees full of ripening oranges and papayas, the sea-rustle of the green-wave, deliciously cold (fresh) matta/underbrush.

Suddenly it's (the line-tree bower, my prison) There, its silent wave/ vibration passing over her, everything Intention/Will, the black yellow butterfly with the red-tipped wings that psychedelics past the bamboo and leaves colour-marks in the air, on her eye, the whole world around her breathing, alive ... if it had a face ...

How did it begin and where did space come from?

"Professora Magda! Professora Magda!"

This high-pitched whine of a voice.

Maria Helena, the Portuguese.

"Professora, are you up there?"

And her face appears over the verandah-edge, the face really not that bad in the afternoon light, the black hair and big eyebrows, black eyes. She looks Greek. You can imagine Medea, Electra ... a shawl around her shoulders, but then she opens her mouth and begins to squeak and it all blows away like smoke.

"I've got the chapter on Baldwin almost finished, and Ellison, I think he's really much more important, more complex. Professor Derrick says that my first chapter that gives the historical background of the identity-problems, that it has to be longer, that it cuts off at the Civil War and ... "

Magda tries to be as electric-fenced as possible. She just wants her to go, go back to Portugal, go back to Angola, just go, not another lecture on ... She hands her a manila folder, and then ...

"Sometimes I just feel it's not worth while. We had so much in Angola. You know my husband was a judge. But here. There's so much fofoca."

"Gossip."

"So much gossip. I never saw such gossip, not in Angola, not in England, not even South Africa ... "

All this autobiography at every meeting. Madga had found it almost interesting the first ... three ... times ... but now ...

She wants it to end. She exudes GO AWAY. And she finally does.

Her thesis on The African Shadow-Identity in Contemporary American Black Writing.

Gone, but the taste (smell) stays on, cold, clouded over, frost-god, fire-god, fern-god, Maria Helena Portuguesa god.

She descends, Nona in the kitchen making coffee. Arms/legs around her, a hungry-god/goddess between her thighs.

"How about a little ... ?"

"Tonight, huh?"

"Nobody here now ... "

"Well ... " turns the edge-of-boiling water off, and they move into the bedroom, Magda goes for between Nona's thighs, tongue anxious, quente/hot, "not that way ... "

The light grey, the electric heater on all day and all night now.

"What's wrong?"

"Let's just use hands ... "

"What's wrong?"

"Can't we just use hands? Does there have to be something always 'oral'?"

"Why not? What's wrong?"

"I'm just not in the mood ... "

"OK ... so ... "

Magda gets up, poncho back on (glimpse of fat black lace frog body in the wall mirror).

"We can do something ... "

"Sometimes," says Magda as she walks out into the kitchen to put the water on again, "sometimes I'd like to have a big fat juicy one inside me, stallion-size, nothing equivocal or ambiguous, just there!"

Not kidding, the rich coffee-smell vapoured up in the steam, whatever it was that made her what she was, she wished it had been "otherwise."


### iv.

Sometimes she (Magda), lying in the bloodless, drained, just-becoming-dawn deadlight, feels menopausically dead. The image is dried insect-bodies/leaves all wind-piled together at the dead end of an autumn walkway next to a brick house just before you come to the unleaved garden.

She knows Nona wants more kids, that she'd (impossibly) like the sperm to be hers.

The impossible (St. Paul) dead-end of all this.

Although, when the night black creams around them, when it's all the same oestrogenic orientation toward almost edematose lazy skin and nipples, and Abstraction is blotted out by the hum of cuddled Now, she doesn't care.

Cycle I's finished. She's given birth three times and now it's Cycle II, wringing from her drying meat whatever wind-music she can ...

In the reviving light eyes hurting less and less.

Accustoming them to the light, then up-thrust into the wrapped-around-robe cold, and the coffee and toast (jam) day begins like a violent after-a-sauna plunge into an icy pond.


### v.

Magda had invited her mother down to Brazil, offered to pay her (guilt) way.

Two weeks later the postman rings.

Dear Magda:

First off I don't need your money. I've been selling the silver, the tea-set, my jewellery, next goes the candelabrum which I've been offered three thousand dollars for. But I can't see myself visiting you in your present condition. When Luis told us you were a homosexual, your father cried. I swear that's what killed him. When I think of all the rest of the family normal, and you such a disgrace, I could just vomit. I can't face the family, I can't face anyone. You with your perfect education and never anything like this in the family. I would rather see you dead than this. How can it be that you kill your father but you don't kill yourself? And to abandon your children the way you have. Thanks anyhow, but I think I'll save myself the ulcers I'd get visiting you, and spend my money on a nice non-buggy trip to Europe instead of Fleabag South America.

Nona in the doorway.

"What does Mirror-Mirror-On-The-Wall have to say?"

"The usual. And it's so hard for me to not feel responsible for Luis going out there and telling them I was gay, and not feel responsible for my father's death, although he'd had his heart-attack ten years before and this ventricular aneurysm he had was paper thin ... and it's hard for me to say I don't give a shit how my cousins live, and fuck family-opinion. And she's selling all the silver she always said I was going to inherit, that evil, egotistical word. It's things I really wanted. And then the dig at South America, that's for Luis ... and the 'Normal.' It's incredible I can still be so hurt ... "

"It really is," says Nona wryly, comes in and sits down on the bed, comforting hand extended to Magda, pulling Magda's head down on her shoulder.

"You must be really pissed off with me," says Magda, "I never seem to learn."

"Not pissed off, bored ... mainly bored with ... I hate to call it your 'stupidity,' although in a sense that's what it is ... or maybe not ... call it wasted hope/optimism ... you demand that she changes, but she won't, she'll always be the same ... "

"Plus the dimension of Sadism which I still have trouble grasping. The pleasure she gets out of it all. I think she must have enjoyed it a lot when my father broke down and cried, and died ... could the news have killed him?"

"Look, he was seventy-five, fat, he'd had an aneurysm for ten years. Besides, what Luis did, he did it, you're not responsible."

"Chata/idiotic, huh?"

"A little … "

Holding on to each other, Magda's all pervading sense of guilt.

Then suddenly she's up, up, up in the sky, the house as house vanishing, becoming this tiny dot far, far below, and the sabre-voice of Mum cutting at her.

"What good are you, really, one daughter, and why you … ?"

Her father's fists descending on her back, crime forgotten, but the punishment never, she wished she'd been there to see him old and with a paper-thin heart, no more fists or punishment, the thin old paper-hearted man weeping, like an old woman, like a kitten.

We move into clouds now, the pinpoint of Magda and Nona on the bed gets lost, out of sight, white, blank, cold, the only sound the meowing-weeping of the old-man kitten …


**vi.**

Magda on the bed. Bedroom = Classroom. And of course she knows she's (black tights, long-sleeved leotard, fringed poncho made out of black velvet) the (so, so carefully thought-out overtones) seductress, without ever moving a thigh-muscle, even pretending that it wasn't there at all, the whirlpool between the legs, sucking in and vaporising all Matter that came within range … an initial "testing," small-talk.

"You speak English well … Brazilians in general speak well, I guess it's because Portuguese is so complex. There's hardly an accent in English. Or unexpected accents. Like yours. It's almost Italian … "

"We were Italians two generations back … as a matter of fact … "

"Amazing … (hawk poised lazily over the trees, and then – sighting its prey – the sudden stiletto plunge down) let's talk about MOSTS for a while, shall we. What do you want MOST in the world?"

She hardly hesitates, small and clinically white, unmade-up, at the other end of the bed.

"To get out of Medicine."

"Why?"

"Because it's deshumanizante … "

"How's that?

She laughs.

"In English … ?"

"In English!"

"Bem … white corridors and I'm white … " laughs again, "I can't say it."

"You can."

"It's like way back I was, what, seventeen, engaged, I thought very much in love."

"How old are you now?"

"Thirty-one ... (pause, the wind and the rain outside, the island seems to have broken loose of its moorings and is drifting to the South Pole) ... that's fourteen years ... I could have a fourteen-year-old child. But when I told him I was going into medical school, I mean really going in and not just talking about it. Well, I had an alternative, ou esquecer de medicina ou esquecer dele ... "

"Either forget Medicine or forget him. But what was the problem?"

"Não se ... I don't know."

"I suppose it's just a simple case of machismo, but ... how about opening a clinic on the island, call it after Dante: VITA NUOVA, NEW LIFE. Plastic surgery accompanied by diet, exercise and yoga. Death-Meditations. Make them look young and then we get them used to the idea that they're going to die. A course in realism. Kübler-Ross, she's this specialist on getting people ready for death. Death-acceptance lessons. So plastic surgery doesn't become escape but an exercise in the frailty of flesh ... "

"Frei ... "

"Fragilidade ... frailty ... "

"You've got this Spanish accent?" she asks tentatively.

"It's my cross," says Magda, "I was married to this Bolivian for fourteen years, and then ... "

"The girls?"

"They're Nona's. My three are all big now, my son's twenty-three... " stops, you can hear the water bubbling and torrenting down the street now, "What's that?"

Out of the (other) bedroom window you can see the flood coming down. It's not a street any more but a violent river.

"I can't believe it," says Bernadette.

"You can stay here tonight, you're never going to be able to drive in that ... you know (facing each other in the dark room, Nona out reading in the living room, with the kids watching TV), when you asked me about children, what I wanted to say is I don't have any, never had any, I was afraid they'd come out spiders."


## vii.

It was noticeable, even after the first week, in the paradoxical congealed green of the tropical winter always reaching down to but never touching zero, that Bernadette was becoming Night too.

New shoes from a place called Hippopotamus.

"Feito sob medida!"

"Made to order," translates Magda, fingers the (black) suede spiked heel, "nice ... the ankle strap (fingers around her thin chicken-ankle) bondage ... "

"Como?"

"The attractiveness of slavery because it eliminates the anguish of choice, especially if it's feigned ... "

"Fay ... ?"

"Fingindo ... and the net stockings. Net as net. Simply that (Magda ready with Cinzano Tinto tonight, two small shot glasses, pour, sip, they settle back warmly sleepy against enormous pillows) how about 'home,' 'growing up' ... I'm curious why you even went into Medicine in the first place ... "

"I suppose I had to 'go into' something. Out of the nine, seven 'went into' something. And the other two ... well, Ze's an accountant. Teresa's a full-time mother. I guess poverty ... "

"How poor were you?"

"My father was a public funcionario/civil servant. We got along but (closing her eyes, purple metallic lids, Magda thinks of her – cadaver-skin, grenadine lips, this fluff of black hair – not as medicine any more, but Cabaret, Groz, Germany, 1933) ... I'm hearing whispers, my father and mother, money-whispers, there's never enough, there's never enough, there's never enough, they're always on the brink of disaster, inside anguish. So they send me to Coração de Jesús which is the snob school in town. And after the holidays everyone comes back with travel-stories and everything, new clothes, jewellery, and I'm inside anguish, on the brink of disaster. You get infected by it ... "

"And Medicine?"

"One brother who's a doctor. And it could have been good."

"If ... ?"

"Despersonaliza ... it ... "

"Depersonalizes ... "

"You become 'function.' You no longer have a face. You're really not a person. And then there's THE HORROR. Like last week I started working on what I thought might be a little tumour between the top of the nose and the forehead. Only I kept going in, in, in and it was inside the whole nose, reached back behind the eyes. I worked on it there, the eyes started getting loose in their sockets. The tumour had worked its way up into the bone under the forehead, was up into the brain. I couldn't get it all without killing him right on the table, so I left what I had to, and otherwise he's strong, he'll last a long, long time, no nose, hardly any face. After a while it seems to be all wrong. There's no norm, standard, just deviation ... "

"Tiger, tiger, burning bright, in the forests of the night ... "

"Tiger?"

"It's a poem about God by William Blake. God as lamb, God as tiger. Pre-Darwin ... "

"What do you believe in?"

"Catholic to ex-Catholic to ... I don't know. I can't believe in an automatic self-generating mindless universe, can I? There's Presence, Cobra-Presence, Tiger-Presence, Lamb-Presence, Cancer-Presence ... but Presence ... only if I try to conform to the contours of the Will out there, the Will out there obviously has nothing to do with the benign. My malignant me begins to shape itself to the dictates of what it's dictating, but what *it's* dictating doesn't have anything to do with the Sermon on the Mount, although it might have to do with obsidian Mexico and Xipe Totec, the Flayed God ... "

"Xipe Totec ... ?"

"It was a thing the Aztecs used to do, the priests would wear the skin of the victim, laced up in the back. It's the vision of Anahuac, Cortes walking into snake-god temples with blood-covered walls, human hearts burning in front of giant snake-god idols. Now there I think you're getting close to your Cancer God, the God Of Horror!"

Another round of Cinzano Tinto, heavy, sweet blood, the heater's on the floor, but the cold South Pole wind rattling through the cracks around the windows, lifts the room up out of the house and rockets it through the upper chill night air.

"A blanket, OK?"

And Magda takes out this huge black fake-fur blanket, covers them both up. Nona sticks her head in the door.

"Tea or coffee?"

"Not for me," says Bernadette.

"Coffee for me," says Magda, and then when Nona's busily in the kitchen, "I tried God as husband-wife for fourteen rotten years, and then she came along and all of a sudden before I knew it I was part of the Adversary God where the rules come from inside out and the only design seems to be hypodermic fangs pumping beyond joy into victim flesh. I get down to the ground of my Being and listen, 'What do you want? What do you really want?' And it talks to me and I'm at home in this spider-jaguar jungle ... "

Soft blanket rolled around them, waves of black within black, soft warm nylon blanket surf and legs. But they don't touch ... poles apart ... waiting for the appearance of the coffee.

## viii.

"When the first one walked out on me, I became não sei, quasi foetal. I wanted to make myself as small and anonymous as possible … "

(curved warm in amniotic darkness)

"But that wasn't the end of … "

"I had 'affairs,' one with an unhappily married man. Aren't they always? Love, but you spend most of your time hearing about the Other One until she's more real than he is, and you almost begin to take her side, whatever that may be, there he is impotentemente … "

"Impotently … "

"Im-po-tent-ly … on the bed next to you. And you think that if he gives her as much love as he gives you, who can blame her for being full-time a fat … como é … reclamadora … ?"

"Fat bitch … "

"Bitch?"

"In Spanish it's perra, but in English it's bitch. Like someone who bitches, complains … "

Looking so medical tonight, even medicinal white shoes, and her face all drawn-up, pinched, like she was going to swallow it right down her whirlpool mouth.

"How was surgery today?"

"Burn patient. Child. Face. Three hours. But then the I.N.P.S… "

"What's that?"

"Like socialised Medicine, I suppose. There's these endless forms. The theatre of the absurd. One mole six hundred Cruzeiros, two moles seven hundred. If the mole's on the face it's more than a mole on the body, and a nose-job is a thousand. That's the same as five moles. There's this whole theatre of the absurd list, and papers, papers, papers to fill out. I wouldn't mind just going into the surgery, but … "

"You've got this 'receptionist'/nurse working for you and Carmen, right? Why don't you train her to do the paperwork?"

"The director of the hospital won't let her in, but on the other hand the papers can't leave the hospital."

"Is it a 'male' thing?"

(Her face a blank white cloud floating through a black existential sky)

"Not really, not a 'specific' male thing, although the whole system in a way's male. Abstractly absurd, unlinked to real 'cases,' people. A virtuoso six hour job gets paid the same as a simple, elementary one hour job. The bureaucratic system's 'male,' isn't it? I mean how many women philosophers have there been in the history of philosophy? And I keep thinking uteruses, breasts, they're there to be used, but … it's like I never make it out of the knife-world, the formulario world. There's no ME any

15

more. I keep wondering how my child/children would have been. And then I project out to the future and where does that go? I'm fifty, sixty, my father's dead. I guess he has to die, and I get the house, I guess, and I've gone through three more dogs. And the money keeps dissolving ... "

She stops. A little more wine.

During the day there's the paradox of bright sun, jade bamboo, emerald persimmon leaves, malachite palms, and wind-sheets of bright (disguised) antarctic cold. But at night the island sails into mute, drained death. They both huddle under their fake black fur.

"I wanted to talk about NOWISM," says Magda, "that's ME, Now, the why of the tights, the soft stuff, because soft-tight says NOW, the why of the Arts, time-out, drop-out, separate-out ... you've lost 'separateness,' there's only a full-time 'drowned' you. Only I feel like such a klutz sermonizing on. As if I were Answers and not just Questions."

They sit quietly now until language becomes silence and waiting, until language becomes wind and cold tourmaline green, the language of a cold heater and numb legs, a tentative approximation of psychic oneness.

"Sometimes I think you're a nun," says Magda, "you're a character out of Mauriac fighting God, Flesh is pretend and your real genetic destiny is to drown in Spirit ... "

"When I was younger, young, younger, young-est, I was all music, art, dance. I wanted to be a musician-artist-dancer, full-time tights and tranças ... "

"A pony-tail."

"Pony-tail?"

"Rabo de cavalo ... "

"But you get the picture, all muscle, legs, body, walking as ... walking as orgasm. Only you're on an island off the coast of Southern Brazil. The ambience isn't ... São Paulo afterwards, when I was doing my plastic surgery residency. Avenida Paulista, the night, espalha electricidade ... "

"Espalha ... scatters electricity ... "

"You know what I mean, though ... ?"

"You mean money, clothes, clothes, money, black-night, pin-point lights, everyone in their gladdest rags, I think thin black nyloned ankles and high-heeled sandalled feet. It's high civilization overspill. It's what all the factories and fazendas are about, they all funnel down to a pair of dying swan white legs ... "

"Only here ... "

"Like me in Chicago. I would have gone into cinematography if there'd been any cinematography, but there wasn't any such animal ... "

Bernadette's English Class Notebook on the bed, Magda's handwriting:

Techniques of a NOWIST; separate time ... take out time daily, Delius,

Debussy, especially the piano works, Mahler.

And then a transcription (in Bernadette's hand) of an Alberto Nepomuceno song, lyrics by Juvenal Galeno:

Medroso de Amor
Moreninha
Não sorrias com meiguice
com ternura
Não sorrias com meiguice
Este sorriso de cantaro não desforres
Não sorrias que eu tenho medo de amores
que só trazem desventuras
Moreninha
Não me fites como agora
Apaixonada,
Não me evites, como agora Moreninha ...

(Moreninha – Brunette, dark, small, don't smile with sweetness, with tenderness, don't smile with sweetness, this singer's smile, don't punish me, don't laugh at me that I'm afraid of loves that bring pain, Moreninha, don't stare at me, like now, passionately, don't avoid me like now ... Moreninha ... )

The garden's closed off, 1890-1910, the long world-autumn before the winter of World War One, the leaves fall slowly, the ground is filled, urns, flagstone walks, the air damp, filled with the sweet-sour odour of resinous decay. Socioeconomics, bayonets and white crosses disappear. It's all heart, surface, the insect-wing fragility of dry, falling leaves ...

### ix.

"No, really," says Magda, she has this habit after meals of getting up from the table altogether and sitting in this big easy-chair, "sometimes I think I became what I am, not as the result of psychological-genetic 'slanting', but because of social conditioning. I mean I learned how to hate men by having contact with them. Although, honestly, when I think of all the quicky, raw-boned, football-duckhunter sex I've had in my life, orgasm as ejaculation instead of the long leap out into space and the slow ground-out-from-under-you-glide-down-to-the-beach again ... it's almost as if instincts ... I keep thinking of St. Paul and the 'unnatural' Roman world that he changed over to the 'naturalness' of Judeo-Christianity, that Kaballistic Jewish-Christian mania for the Word divorced from the Thing, the Perjorative Rule, always the prescriptive instead of descriptive, as if the purpose of life was to bend away from Nature, anti-instinct, instead of just hanging loose … "

"That's a funny image for you to use," says Nona.

"Isn't it … "

And she's up for just one last crumb of whole wheat bread oozing with butter and almost-oily sweet guava jam.

**x.**

"You ought to become a dancer now, if you want," says Magda.

"I don't know … sometimes I feel it's all so 'late' for me … "

"I wish Anaïs Nin hadn't died … "

"Who?"

"Writer … American, I guess you'd call her American. This perfect doll face glued on the time-wall of white muslin. But she only made it to, what, 65, 67 … I wanted her to make it to 90, still the same face. And then transfigure, not a wooden box in a concrete vault, but some sort of 'resurrection.'"

Bernadette's (permanently?) different tonight, black mesh legs, boots. Magda touches the leather.

"God, they're soft."

"Camurça de porco."

"Pigskin suede."

"From The Hippopotamus."

"You'll have to give me the address, I'd like to get a pair."

"I'd like to have a black suede body."

This almost-black purple lipstick tonight, this black-fringed scarf turbanned around her head, her pterodactyl thin face, the tighter the head-'form' the better.

Magda touches the fringe.

"Beautiful … "

Not just simple fringe but gathered in fanning-out bunches of five strands.

"It was my grandmother's."

Magda wondering, you reach back sixty, seventy years, the tail-end of the Belle Epoque. Lace-patterned technology at the service of lying on your back shadowed in the heavy metal hues of World Autumn. Le Grande Illusion.

"And the necklace?" rhomboid beads of, "What is it?"

"Onyx, my grandmother's too … "

"The picture begins to form. The elegance of black silk-satin, the body laced, under-cover … laced shoes/boots, the black stockings, corsets

18

... everything that today we consider sado-masochistic, all part of the everyday of love. And then it shifts into helmets and puttees, mustard gas, gas-chambers ... "

Nona sticks her head in, coffee on a tray.

"Could I join you?"

"Come on in."

The Black Topaze Chamber.

Coffee all around.

"Don't let me interrupt," says Nona.

"You wonder why such vehemence against the Zoroastrian, Manichee, Albigensian, Orthodox Anti-Ecstatics, the Church as the Middle Way, Sanity. But REALITY, what's sane about REAL REALITY, what was sane about our first marriages ... the indifferent male dagger in you full-time ... "

Nona reaches down into a bag next to the bed, pulls out a sweater she's making.

"So you know how to tricotar?"

"Knit," says Magda, writes it down in Bernadette's notebook.

"That's really all I like to do," says Nona, "in fact I'd like to open a business, get out of the university altogether ... "

Magda up tight all of a sudden, the rich eroticism suddenly replaced by THEM plotting, numbers and 'success' ...

"I wanted to talk a little about the anti-Christ," she says.

"So talk," says Nona, and she does, this world, this flesh, this pleasure, moment, the desperate, one-time-around evaporating impulse NOW, but the whole time she's watching Bernadette's static hands, knitting in time, tied to (forever) Nona.

Knitting her own (the Shroud of Turin) shroud.


**xi.**

"I feel like ... like I did when I was twelve ... you don't have an image of yourself so you keep looking in the mirror trying to find one ... definir-se ... "

Bernadette is so incense and crystal-balls tonight, purple lizard eyelids, her body a soft black-velvet purr.

"And what's emerging?" asks Magda, Nona (significantly) next to Bernadette at the foot of the bed, Magda at the head.

"I'm not a doctor, and I'm not a physical therapist, and I'm not in Canada with my brother, Luiz, I'm not, not, not ... "

"What I was thinking," says Milk-white Nona, knitting Christmas sweaters (cold-moving-into-spring-August) for her nieces in Kansas

City, "is that she might come back to the US with us. We could open a store. You know, Carlos, the gemcutter, well, I talked to him this week about lessons in cutting and he said OK, he's never done it before, but … "

"You've been busy, huh?" says Magda, addressing herself to Bernadette's obvious uncomfortableness, "Look, I give her certain things, I give her what I can, but there's certain things I don't have to give, friends and lovers, lover, OK, but there's a certain lizardishness about me. Out of the window in my hotel room in João Pessoa, a whole colony of small grey iguanas perched at various places on the wall, waiting for lunch to fly by. Only I don't knit. You've got to reconstruct the kitchen of Nona's childhood … there's the big table, Mum, Grandma, maybe Aunt Mabel, Grandma's sister, maybe Jean and Martha, the sisters, there's cookies, coffee, Dad and Brother Bill in the living-room watching football, and the women are all talking about, well, maybe they're talking about Bill's first wife, Darlene, his son, Douglas, who's not doing too well in school because Darlene's always got these lousy jobs because she never finished college. I mean just missed by two courses, but the degree keeps moving away from her down the night-tracks, it's not two courses any more, but five, and the rules are changed and maybe Darlene's there, she's got a job at an ad agency and 'Jim's after me to work every night, and I don't trust him, and anyhow, the payroll was late last month and we've lost a ton of clients, and where's the money gonna come from anyhow … ?' She's white-trash, hick, hayseed … "

"Não estou entendendo nada/I'm not understanding anything … "

"She's caipira, she's a caipira in spite of all her My Fair Lady self-improvement sophistication. There's still the twang … "

"Twa … ?"

"Sotaque, sabor … the point being that that's her tribal group. And me, I was an only child isolated in a Yardley lavendered room by myself, never on the 'making' but always on the 'taking' end of things … " adds Magda.

"What she wants to say," says Nona, "is that she's The Great Lady Spectator, isolated and served, and I'm the Integrated Servant … "

"I'm psychologically 'cold,'" says Magda, "you're psychologically 'warm.' I'm not comfortable in the Kansas City Hen-nery … "

"Hen…?"

"Galinheiro."

"And what makes you think I would be … ?"

"I've seen you with Bettina, Nazaré, Teresa … here … your hands even want to knit, don't they, I mean they are knitting without your even wanting them to … "

Bernadette laughs, guiltily, knits air with imaginary needles, then settles back and her eyes turn into swimming globes of visionary crystal.

"As long as we're just 'free-associating', what about visas ... and I'd like to have a child. That's the one terrible thing about 'your', I almost said 'our' kind of marriage ... and it's like I believe in function so deeply ... "

"I never thought I'd hear the Natural Law defended by those purple gypsy lips," sarcasms Magda, Bernadette retreating, all the black closet doors, the black drapes over the high, dark, grey-shuttered windows quietly and secretly close, "I'm just kidding ... although I tell you one thing I've really come to believe in, the Fatherless Child. You have your baby without the agony of a marriage, which is either going to end up in a divorce or life-imprisonment anyhow. You choose the man and the moment, and just do it. The end-result, your business ... "

Then (Magda) stepping out of herself, back to the Sound and the Fury, In the Midst of (Hot) Life, out of the astroid cold where she'd been, looking down at Earth from the other side of (empty) Death, wondering, all the arrumando/fixing things up for what ... you could just as well cross your arms and legs and do NOTHING full (beyond traitor Maya-Illusion) Time.


## xii.

"You see I can't leave Medicine and stay here," she says, full moon night on the sails of the island world. She varies back and forth, seductress to autoclave, tonight inappropriately autoclave. Centrifuged down to the raw pulp of fear/disgust.

"Why not?" devil-advocates Nona.

"There's padrões de comportamento ... "

"Behaviour patterns," translates Magda.

"Behaviour pat-terns ... you get married and you're 'released', marriage is accepted/acceptable. Only as long as you're not married, you're the baby-sitter for whoever needs sitting, the bank for whoever needs doctoring. That's ... "

"Built in ... " suggests Madga.

"Built in?"

"Inerente, embutida ... "

"Built in ... "

"So come back with us, period. Look, I've had my Ph.D. for what, almost ten years, and NOTHING PERMANENT. Not that there's no jobs, only they've got to hire blacks now ... " Nona whines.

"Guy from the Detroit slums with a Ph.D. from Harvard. When they hired him I called up Henry, the boss, and said 'Listen, out of a hundred and twenty-six people in the department, when you got 'elected' there were ten against you, which meant me and my friends. You bypass Nona

21

in the hiring process now and you're gonna feel it. So he invites us over for dinner. There he is, Detroit with Harvard manners. And not feigned either. Added. But permanently, silver plate ... there he is with this pink-blonde psychiatrist, all cutesy-pooh and perfect ... "

"Bastard world," says Nona, knitting purses now. They're both knitting purses, the Act precedes the Theory, the Do precedes the Why.

Out of cotton string, pulling Spring in on the end of cotton string, and Bernadette's enamoured of purple and green dyes, reduplicating the Highlands, the Joyce Country in Ireland in the tropical South Atlantic.

"It's a blessing I wasn't taken 'in,'" continued Nona, reaching, reaching, reaching – into the interior vision, "I'll tell you what it is ... it's like the hospital, rectangular, there's the round buttocks 'real'-world and then the surreal straight-line manstructures that people begin to take for real so they really become The Role themselves. I keep seeing Joyce Rudell and Jocelyn Tien ... "

"Como é ... ?" asks Bernadette.

"Two members of the department up there, like built-in dowdy ... "

"Dow ... ?"

"Desarrumada," supplied Magda, "professionalmente desarrumada ... "

"I keep seeing them over at Jacobson's tearoom having tuna fish salad in a tomato-shell, lunches on stage, inside 'role.'"

Night invades the Black Topaze Chamber. Magda turns off the light and the moon floods across the bed and their faces white-glow alive.

"I'm thinking of two plays," says Magda, "*Dear Brutus* and *Midsummer Night's Dream*. And Bergman's *Summer Nights*, I forget the title ... the ecstatic Indians who live whole lives centred on VISION. The world swells, drips juice, becomes bilateral, rich labyrinth. It's like the mind needs Datura or Mescal, by itself it loses all the finer-tuning. The world's infra-wild, mystery. Not white hospital, cream-coloured university corridors ... "

The moonlight hums around them, bodies give way to ectoplasmic spirit-forces, Inside oozes delicately-featured Out, the thousand-petalled lotus blooms on their foreheads, cross-legged on the bed factory-time stops, time becomes TIME, even when Magda puts the lights on again and there's this enormous spider on the window screen. She touches its underside with her fingernail and it disappears away, under the Hood of Moon.

"So we open a store?" says Nona.

"OK ... can I get a permanent visa?" asks Bernadette.

"Have you ever been to Hispano-New York. Why not YOU?" says Magda.

### xiii.

Luiz, Bernadette's brother. His wife, Elizete, the one with the big nose and the impeccable, low-key, casual-elegant taste.

It was all just an excuse for a little "therapeutic frenzy."

Elizete was graduating as an electrical engineer, and then they were off to Canada for his Ph.D., and the graduation party was at the Lagoa Yacht Club.

You leave Pantanal, go up over this mountain, toward the sea, and there it is, the Lagoon (Lagoa), it's where the Indians lived before the Portuguese settled the island, where the burial mounds (Sambaqui) are, a huge pendulous breastshaped lagoon, fed by streams and the sea, renovated by the tides, the club built next to it.

Nona makes this black lace little shoulder-strap dress for Magda, calls it "The Classic Classy Whore." She begins with Magda's favourite black slinky thin slip and then builds the black lace on top of that.

Nona has on this pink Jersey pyjama-ish thing that Magda bought her during one of her lecture trips to Rio, and which is in-IN.

Bernadette goes down to Hippopotamus and picks up this black version of Nona's pyjama-ish thing, has a pair of arch-breaker ankle-straps made, goes down to the beauty parlour and has The Works, from nails to lashes, hair like black, scrambled spinach, gets tiny little black lace purses for the three of them.

They descend down the green moonlit Lagoa hills to the Club, show cards/tickets, get inside.

"My god, it's a re-run of a combined Great Gatsby and Last Tycoon," says Magda, "I've never seen so much black jersey, lace, lycra and nylon in one place in my life before … "

Which is when Bernadette notices her purse is gone, little dollface (Stripper, Hooker, but Doctor never!) all screwed up in mainly distrust.

"The evening begins," says Magda, sharing her anguish, and back they go, out of the main gates into the car park.

"Maybe I dropped it when I got out of the car … " into the car, someone passing by goes and gets a flashlight out of his car, they look all over on the sand, trying to re-construct, re-trace, re-member.

Nothing. Back into the Club and she leaves a message with the guy at the gate, "In case anyone finds a purse … " but he hardly pays any attention, they move into the samba-rock sound-crush.

"You can feel your tissues bounce," says Magda.

"I love it," says Nona.

"Me too … " echoes Magda.

Luiz comes and gets Nona, drops her into the boiling crowds, leaving Bernadette and Magda alone.

"Why not?" says Magda, and they clasp together, Giant Magda and Pygmy Bernadette.

"David and Goliath," says Magda.

"Eu gosto/I like it," says Bernadette.

"Me too ... are you OK ... ?"

"Well, I've got the car-keys in the purse, all my IDs, it's such an awful amount of work trying to 're-get' everything. Maybe it'll show up."

"Hope so ... "

Nobody notices them or cares, everyone drunk, gassed, gone, the exploding-out enthusiasm, release. Of course it's worse than the US, the pressure, thinks Magda, here it's either college degrees and the middle class or no degrees and lowest class poverty, the room's full of a sense of escape, relief, triumph. It's the Victory Dance of the Chosen. Bernadette so sweet, puppyish, little girlish, Kewpie Dollish, fofinha/soft that Magda wants to engulf (engolir – devour) her right then and there, out into the car park, down to the Lagoon, under the beowulf water, down to the black nylon jersey pyjamaey eyeless, brainless depths of pure DO.

The structures of cellular ooze. You've gotta see Luiz to believe him, usually as nervous-scared as a cockroach, tonight he's The Flash, The Zoot-Suit Kid, right out of Guys and Dolls, some old Danny Kaye (Wonder Man) film, jumping, jiving, rubber-legs, funny face, with his Chinese mandarin beard and moony black Portuguese eyes, bald on top, long and stringy on the sides.

"Honestly," says Magda when Bernadette's feet start aching and they're sitting down again, swilling a little whiskey, "with that face and that tux, if he started pulling pink elephants out of his sleeves, I wouldn't be surprised."

"Eles Iestão tão contentes porque dentro de muito pouco vão viajar/ they're so happy because within a short time now, they'll be leaving."

"Well, it's still not awful now in October, but if he waits another month ... for Canada, I mean even I used to feel punished in Montreal in April. To move from Green Paradise to six uninterrupted months of White Hell. Dante doesn't have the lowest levels in Hell fiery, but frozen. And I think it fits ... "

"The only thing I'd worry about would be my skin – it even gets red and chapped down here in the middle of winter ... "

"You get used to it. Or you can use protective oil. Or stay inside most of the time. As far as I'm concerned, I'm more made for cold than warm. A hundred thousand years of Neanderthal Middle-Europe. The survival of the sauer-krautist ... "

"O que?"

"Esquece ... forget it ... "

Luiz bringing Nona back, going for Magda, she towers over him, likes him, likes the way he is with Isadora, their baby, with Elizete. Bernadette always on the edge of humour, the tragic vision not allowed to enter.

"You're not neglecting Elizete?" Magda asks as they walk out onto the floor.

"Don't be silly," he answers, "she got a whole turma/class to dance through. She's out of her mind tonight, her parents came down from Brasilia … "

Meu bem voce me da agua na boca/my love, you give me water in my mouth,

Vestindo fantasias, tirando a roupa/wearing fantasies, taking off your clothes …

The vocalist wasn't Rita Lee, but good.

"It's true, everything they say about Brazil."

"Everything bad, you mean."

"The good and the bad. I never expected Paradise, but it's close … "

A gente faz amor por telepatia/we make love by telepathy

He calms down, it's a calm-down song, her dress and lycra-poured legs are caressingly liquid, she doesn't have to prove anything to anyone, feels dead and resurrected into infinite transparency.

"All set for Canada?"

"I don't know, I'm waiting for the TOEFL results … you know, English as a Foreign Language. If I don't get above five hundred, I'll have to go up there just to study English first."

"But you're OK now. For an electrical engineer. If you were studying literature it'd be something else, but … "

No chão, no mar, na lua, na melodia/On the ground, in the sea, in the melody.

"And Bernadette?"

"I want her to take the medical exam and go up as an M.D., but she seems to hate Medicine so much. I thought it'd be fun for us. We could study together. I could use a good course in general medicine."

Nada melhor do que não fazer nada,

So pra deitar e rolar com voce!/Nothing better than not doing anything, only lying down and rolling around with you.

"And what does she say?"

"I don't think she wants to … "

(Exams flying into her head, like bats at sunset, all these impossible multiple-choice questions about amino acids and psychiatry and neurology – "Projectile vomiting indicates … " – and she sits there, "I used to know all this stuff ten, twelve years ago, but … ") Can, but … Magda towering over Luiz. Up there he's going to be so small. She thinks of the small Portuguese conquistadores ... Music over, and suddenly she's at the airport herself, they're all there to see her off, Carmen and the other Bernadette, Hilario, students.

And she's gotta leave Brazil. It's ending.

De tanto a gente se beijar/de tanto imaginar loucuras/People kissing so much, so much imagining crazynesses.

And she's full of tears.

Getting presented to Elizete's parents, the almost English-looking (tidily prim, overwashed) mother, and the father who tries to talk to her in English with the illogic of "I was in Italy during the war ... " (what war's that?)

"Are you OK?" Nona asks.

"I was just thinking about leaving," she explains, "I have these little psychopathic 'flashes.'"

Sits down.

Whiskey.

Qualquer maneira de amor vale o canto
qualquer maneira me vale contar/any form of love is worth the song, however you say it, say it.

The vocalist's OK, but Magda thinks back to soft, black incense-ashes, night-fur Milton Nascimento doing it, Gal Costa, bright porcelain metallic ...

Qualquer maneira de amor valerá/any kind of love is always worth it

Flashes of winter city-streets, Chicago, Cleveland, dry, dead, grey-cemetery cities.

"Me querían contratar mais un ano, com a possibilidade após de ficar para sempre ... they wanted to contract me for another year, with the possibility afterwards of staying on for good," Magda finds herself telling Elizete's father.

"And why don't you do it?" he asks, "If you like it ... "

"I never felt a stranger here. From the first day. The strangest I've felt was confronting the word abacaxi."*

He laughs (put him in a British colonel's uniform and he'd pass ... so 'un-Brazilian').

"It's strange enough."

Elizete comes off the dance-floor in these avocado-coloured "pyjamas," this long aristocratic face glistening with sweat and excitement, Bettina, Bernadette's younger sister, right behind her. Bernadette's bought her a pair of black "pyjamas" for tonight's samba slumber-party too. Milton Nascimento invades Magda's head ...

---

*Abacaxi – Pineapple.

Sergipe, Alagoas, Palmeres,

Ireré,

Yemanjá.

traz notícias,traz noticias de mamãe/bring

news, bring news of The (Great) Mother …

"You look good," Magda tells Bettina, the soft fofinha one, the throwback to soft, cuddleable, cuddling Italian grandmothers.

"Obrigado a Bernadette," she says, "Thanks to Bernadette."

Bernadette hears, smiles, winces.

The Yemanjá sea-goddess of the family, coming from the Sea of Surgery-Earned Money bearing extras, and the pressure is to forever, forever, forever stay, can just see her brothers and sisters and poor widowed father going down the tubes without her. Her surrogate children, her father become her surrogate son.

"Let's dance … "

And Nona and Magda hit the floor.

Começar de novo e contar comigo/beginning again and

taking me in,

Vai valer a pena ter amanhecido/worth the trouble to

have dawned/begun …

Magda wanting beginning again to be infinite, over and over and over again … Juicy Nona, if she'd have her belly-flab removed and her jowls, and the wrinkles around her eyes, she has this Queen Bee body, juiciness, all glands, The Ovary of the World.

Joke on TV (Planeta dos Homens/The Planet of Men) the other night: They're always talking about Brazil as a Sleeping Giant that's starting to wake up … well, how can any giant sleep with an external debt of twenty billion dollars …

"I keep believing," says Magda, Nona a little ashamed of showing the whole world what they really are, she can feel the tension/shame in her body/arms, but Magda's not ashamed, really no one cares, it's ego-night, the end of suffering, finally getting the free ticket to the eternal middle class.

"Believing in what?"

"Body, I don't know … in cockroaches and Jararacas … "**

Nona clicks her tongue, Tsk, tsk.

"What are you talking about now … ?"

"Forget it."

She never thought she'd be coming "back" to the Stations of the Cross via negative-"design."

** Jararaca – a deadly poisonous snake in Brazil.

Sonhe com un sonho, que ninguem sonhara/

I dream a dream that no one else dreams …

3:45, they stagger out past the main gate and Bernadette asks again, "There wasn't a purse left here was there?"

"As a matter of fact," and he pulls it off a shelf, the cord cut, she goes into it.

"All the documents, no money."

"You mean to say it was stolen in this regal atmosphere?" Luiz sneers, goes into his pocket, fifty Cruzeiros for the guy at the gate.

"Come on, let's go back, we've gotta celebrate this."

"I'm so 'heavy,'" says Magda, something inside her afraid of the approach of twittering, cool-winged dawn.

"Come on," everyone together vamos, vamos, vamos … Luiz drags out his last Cruzeiros (in the dining-room/bar), calls over the waiter, "Is there enough here for shrimp and beer?"

"For beer, yes, for shrimp, no … "

"Just a little plate … "

"Well … "

And they get a nice plate of shrimp, more beer. He's 'gone,' Elizete's out, Bernadette wide-awake in stocking feet (black-dotted tights), Nona's asthmatically drowsy, nodding, dozing, Magda revives, dawn is in the air, it's been so long since she's lasted a night until dawn.

Sky-earth-water stirring, rippling, fluttering, twitching awake. Luiz going on about how he's going to let his beard grow long enough to pull it up on top of his head to keep him warm in Canada.

Magda gets up, he doesn't even notice, three waiters hovering, waiting for them – the last ones in the dining room/bar – to finish, but enjoying watching Luiz in action.

Magda outside, Bernadette behind, then beside her.

"Incrível /incredible!"

Over the lagoon from behind the hills the yellow plume-fire ball of the sun, and the moon right next to/above it, crescent moon and blooming sun, unreal hung side by side, the rush of bird-wings over them, wind cold, still winter, arms around each other, skin responding through the touch of layers of lycra and nylon, hands suddenly exploring, touching, bodies together, you could hear Luiz in the background, beyond the breezy flap of banana leaves.

"Not here," says Bernadette, her tongue suddenly springing into Magda's mouth.

"Not here … "

And later, back home, after Sonia and Antonio and their kids have been taken home, they all get into Magda's big bed, Madga in the middle, full day now softened into cold veiling grey, exhaustion slowly disappears, Force/Potency enters into the room and works up their thighs, they both have Magda, Magda has them, The Power and the Glory rip through the room almost without forethought.

Afterwards, that afternoon, Bernadette says "I don't like it all three together. I like more exclusivity/privacy … " but the grey rush-of-waves-moment hangs over them all day, memory-hands still touch memory-thighs/-groins/-breaths, muted, mummy-swatched in soft nostalgia, under the simultaneity of sun-moon-stars, the three of them slowly becoming night-bichos/bugs to whom day is a pallid nuisance.

### xiv.

It stopped being just Friday.

SOL DA TERRA – EARTH-SUN … Nona and Magda had passed by lots of times, but now it became centre: whole wheat crunchy pizza, and whole wheat cakes gooey with bananas and oranges, Prata do Dia, Today's Plate, always whole rice with soya protein, salad, a cigar-shaped whole wheat kibe … and the juices, orange, papaya, maracujá, banana, a whole macrobiotic store on the first floor. Alexandra didn't like any of the stuff at SOL DA TERRA, not even the cakes. So they usually stopped and got her a cheeseburger first. It never bothered her being a Carnivore Sinner in the Holy Land of Macrobiotic. In fact, Alexandra, you don't want to call her insensitive, but inertial-guidance self-directed, this stocky body, big shoulders, beautifully German Shepherd rich hair and these enormous black eyes like her mother (large economy-size Puerto Rican whore, Magda always thought, when she was ecstacising on her back in the parchment candlelight), she'd sit in Macrobioticland munching stolidly on meat. The others were wrong, she was infallibly RIGHT.

Marge, on the other hand, shovelling in the Prato do Dia with her wide Bohemian eyes (Nona's husband had been Czech-American … like Magda) and her fine, long brown-blonde hair, sensitive, reacting-interacting always with the boohs and yeahs around her, never really quite sure of her-SELF … seven (Marge) and five (Alex).

"I don't know what the influence of 'us' is going to be on them," says Magda, munching into a rich, crumbly piece of banana cake, which is all she has ("Line!") most of the time, although when does she stop at one piece … ?

"When I look around me," says Nona, "at 'normal' marriages … like my sister, Jean, she 'endures' her husband, I mean 'endures' his heaviness, his saving-statistics, insurance-statistics, his Number Mind, his football, his … like there was this convention out in Denver and he was thinking about bringing her along with him, it would have cost him, I don't know, five dollars a day extra, something like that, and there was some kind of special on the air-fare … "

"Air-fare … ?"

"Tarifa," translates Magda.

"Un Casal durante a semana, a couple during the week, paga uma metade, pays half-price," explains Nona, her accent in a way better than Magda's for all of Magda's facility. Nona has no Spanish 'underlayer,' just Portuguese. Nothing to un-learn. Just to learn. "And he debated on and on about it, like, god she really wanted to go at first, at the end she just wouldn't, it was less painful to just stay at home … "

"Isn't it true," says Bernadette, sipping down her papaya-banana juice in small measured gulps, "isn't it true that homosexuals always come from 'normal' families … ?"

"What I see," says Magda, "is the Perennial Male, there he is, the Silver-Backed Bore, invincibly ignorant in his maleness, inexorably hooked to the Eternal Football Game, the Eternal Duck-Hunt, the Eternal Heavyhand, brutality, or if not brutality, then, football-skin thick sensibilities … " her voice and adrenalin up.

"You really mean it, don't you?" Bernadette amused.

"He's always in front of me," says Magda, "no, that's not true, but when I do invoke him … his thing was real-estate … he loved/loves to go around and collect rents and check out failing furnaces and leaking roofs. They're his babies, they're him, penis-extensions, property is orgasm, rent ejaculation, he's able to completely substitute the Out There for his own body. Hit and run … "

"Hit and … ?" asks Bernadette.

"That's his sex-life. Choca e corre. The only point of having a body is to support brain and prick."

"Prick?"

"Membro."

"A lot of people here speak English," says Nona.

"Sorry … "

But she's not. Banana-orange, it couldn't be thicker, and her tongue expertly nudges into the juicy wet mass of the cake.

"You're never sorry," says Nona.

"But I try … "

**xv.**

Sonia took the message, scrawled on a pad on Magda's desk:

Quero falar com voce urgentamente/I urgently want to talk to you.
Bernadette

It must be Boss Bernadette (who else?) so she calls her office.

"No, I didn't leave any message, it must be Bernadette Lunardelli, she's doing an article for *Jornal da Semana* about 'foreigners' in Santa Catarina … "

"OK."

So maybe I oughta call her Magda thinks, but she doesn't, the next evening this almost-middle-aged moonface appears at the door.

"I just took a chance you might be home … "

And in she comes, the other Bernadette, and Nona is on Magda's bed reading (English lesson) *Wuthering Heights*, toasty (heater) warm, all three of them in black tights and ponchos as if they were a uniform, all these black-veiled thighs.

"How do you like it down here?" Bernadette reporter asks Bernadette and Nona.

"OK, except for the bichos/bugs," answers Nona.

"We can talk in the living room," says Magda slightly … the word in Portuguese is 'exaltada'/hysterical-happy.

"You three live together?"

"Bernadette, the little one, she's not really 'living' with us yet full-time, but she will be … after she leaves Medicine … "

"Oh, she's a doctor going to leave Medicine? Another American?"

"No, Brazilian … "

"But you and the … "

"We've been together for more than ten years now … "

"Together?" She's shamelessly (reportorially) curious.

"Off the record," says Magda pointing to Bernadette's notepad/pen, "I mean really off the record. I don't want my job jeopardized."

"Of course, of course," she answers, her face all solicitously contorted with 'secrecy,' 'discretion.'

"Well, we were both unhappily married, her for four and me for fourteen years, we never had had anything like this before, perfectly 'normal' and all that. Well, you know, impulses, closet-thoughts. The English department 'gave' her to me as a 'reader,' essentially paper-grader, a luxury we don't have any more. And we started having coffee together every morning, and then it was lunch, and then our husbands were both out of town on this weekend, she came over to my place, it was Autumn, fire in the fireplace, hot buttered rum … rum quente com manteiga e açucar … the kids upstairs asleep, you've got this cumulative horniness anyhow, after ten years of non-marriage, drink a little, you've got a body that cries for responding to and has never really been responded to 'properly,' it's been brutalized but never really been adequately 'loved,' in fact since then I've come to feel (thinking I shouldn't talk, I shouldn't open up, can I trust that face, those eyes, but Inertia taking over, a kind of aggressive, frontal-attack JOY) that the Male can never really adequately love the Female, the whole body-orientation/sensibility's so alien … "

"Well," (she giggles nervously), "I don't know … "

(Never will)

"So anyhow, now it looks like we're three instead of two … "

"Just as long as you don't become a colony like Jim Jones in Guiana … OK … let me see," and she opens her notebook again.

"I've got three grown children from my first marriage, only she didn't have any … "

"So … " she starts to write.

"Just one second more of off the record, OK … ?"

Stops again.

"Well, she wanted to have children, right? And she's got two, a Spaniard eight years ago in Madrid, and six years ago a Londoner … "

"I don't know if I understand … "

"If we're both working, we neither want nor need men, except as, you know, sperm-banks … "

"But they're 'illegitimate' then."

"Which could have been a problem a hundred years ago, but now, who asks, gives a damn … "

She's thinking, "feeling," no, it's not working for her, this time the notebook and pen are claws for getting out of sandholes, sand traps, fast …

"Your accent … ?"

"Well, my first husband was Peruvian, so … "

"Do you find it helps you here?"

"Everyone takes me for an Argentinian, which isn't particularly good, particularly in a hate-Argentinian area … "

"Something which I've never really understood."

"Well, it's a great nation in decline. I should say already declined. All the culture, buildings, pretence, the dream fulfilled somewhere around 1925. And then physically (economically) dissolved, while the esprit stays on … soured … "

"How do you feel about Brazil?"

"Off or on the record … ?"

Pen stops again.

"Off."

"OK ... under the Myth of Cordiality, I think the cordiality's really there, but like Brizola said the other day, it's a conspiracy of the military dictatorship plus the Brazilian moneyed-people plus the multinationals, conspiring to keep it all 'down,' 'controlled,' 'poor.' Brazil has been ... anything outside Rio and São Paulo, has been isolated in the Time Museum. Only now with TV, radio, media, suddenly space is eliminated and it all becomes simultaneous. There's no Out There, it could all be suddenly NOW, only that might mean the levelling that's been going on in the rest of the world for the last hundred years might invade here and that wouldn't do, I mean for the Money and the Military ... "

"You sound like a Socialist," she tentatively volunteers.

"I was a Catholic, which – as all military dictators know – can be a dangerous revolutionary force if you're honest about it. The dishonest Catholic, of course, kisses Caesar's arse ... "

"Como?"

"Beja o cu de Cesar ... "

Nervous titter, just a touch of indignation/The Censor.

"And the people here?"

"There's this one trait about them that makes them really different, they're genuinely sybarites ... "

"Siba ... ?"

"Lotus-eaters, ecstatics, they really are groin and glands. Of course there's this huge difference between Sertão and Coast. The Sertão's the last bastian of Abstract Justice, Our Lady of the Head, as if the Abstract moved inland and the Body stayed on the coast. But if you get one hundred percent inflation and don't subsidise rice and beans, then, even if you stay Body, the Body becomes pain, not pleasure, becomes kill instead of fuck ... "

"O que?"

"Foder, matar em vez de foder ... no, I used to really be a serious Catholic, Czech-Irish Chicago, slum-worker. In a way it's not that Christlike, the Poor aren't the Blessed but the Damned, and you, the social worker, become the Saviour. If you were really Christian you'd accept the poor/poverty, maybe cure, but not preach the Kingdom of God in Appliances. I mean BLESSED ARE THOSE WHO LIVE AND DIE THINKING SOLELY OF KINGDOM COME. Christ and Satan on the mountain. 'My Kingdom is elsewhere.' Other-worldliness. Which is OK as long as you have an uncorrupted poor, but the Brazilian poor aren't ... "

"Were they ever?"

"In Africa before they came over, maybe on the old slave plantations ... I'm thinking of Nabuco's lament in Minha Formação for the lost loyalties of the old fazendas ... but all that implies subsistence-thinking, or you might even call it Poverty Existentialism (singing in English), I've Got the Sun in the Morning and the Moon at Night ... "

"Como? Não entendo muito bem o ingles ... "

"Porgy and Bess, a white man's imagined version of a non-consumerist black man. Only you create the market as the temple, and then cut buying power down to below subsistence, and you've got Black Boy Killers ... "

"Só os pretos? Only the blacks?"

"Richard Wright's Black Boy, but it can just as well be White Boy or Brown Boy, not so much Yellow Boy because you've got your own sub-culture world where you're not marginal. The more 'integrated' you get, the more you leave origins, and then you're glaringly out in the open – unmoored, floating, 'marginal,' that's the beautiful term, 'marginal' ...."

"And the US in all this?"

"Let's talk about US vulnerability. As long as we're in the Balance of Payment world someone's gotta lose, and even in Keynesylandia fantasy-money has to have some foundation somewhere ... so if the balance doesn't tilt in the US's favour in South America ... it's our 'sphere,' isn't it?"

"But how much does it contribute to perennial impoverishment?"

"Well, take the multinationals out and back in come the colonials. If you could have national democracy ... "

"You don't think the multinational presence keeps the structure stratified?"

"I think Dom Pedro II ... that 'upper'-/snob-classism is built into Brazil, 'level' and the Lords of Creation lose their glitter. Anything but that, huh?"

"And the future?"

"It's a little late for the storming of the Planalto Palace, isn't it? I mean it's like 1917 isn't likely to return, you don't have a well-intentioned sealed-in-on-themselves Czar and Czarina and an army distracted by an external war. You can't discount the effects of the 'Western' war on the October Revolution. Here you've got a very alert, 'in touch' military, and 'peace,' even if it is with an iron-fist around your throat ... change that, I mean suddenly destabilise the frontiers, or let the military high command lose touch with the Army as such ... of course that's even a tradition, isn't it, the isolated N.E. rebel (Canudos – Conselheiro) ... ? To expect a Lenin or a Castro to come out of the Brazilian tropicalistic sambaistic middle class ... it's almost as if you have to import your tortured existentialists like Clarice Lispector ... "

Magda loves it. It's as if all the book-years suddenly take on flesh, glow warm.

She's Head in a setting of rich, warm, secretory Meat. She knows they're "listening" and being impressed, the reporter's impressed, she's American, after all, woman, even the Spanish-pimentoed Portugués is at least fluent. And to know what she knows about Brazil, when all her compatriots (like Derrick) are down here for years and they can't even ask for a beer …

## xvi.

The Coordinates of Night, as the island sails into dream, are emerald praying mantises ferocious against the bathroom window, and the moaning of lost-Indio bamboo, owls and rabbits, the cobra-slide-hush through wet grass. When the antarctic rain comes, the island swells and drowns and you'd think it would melt down and wash away into the sea. But it doesn't, and rooster dawn rains on, the green gets greener, you sink further and further down into catatonic aristocratic escape.

The Outside disappears and you swim in the pure green-black of essential Self.

## xvii.

Magda with an old copy of December in hand, picture of Carol Doda, Bernadette's said she thinks the silicon breasts are funny/ridiculous, and Nona agrees.

Old Man Winter night-talking through the green, frost in São Paulo, Paraná, Minas Gerais, sometimes you feel its fingers have to touch here, but they never do.

"I like them," says Magda about Carol Doda's breasts, "even if they are dangerous, I'd trade with her … and the waist and the face … look how the skin's pulled up tight over the skull … "

"Skull?" Bernadette crosses her eyes and re-explodes it, "Skkkkull … "

"Cheek-bones … "

"No, I like skkkull," she says, "skull, murder, spook, squash … smash … que joia/how great … "

"And bushiganga, missanga, paralelopípedos … Portuguese is in no position to make fun of anyone else," says Nona.

"But we lack, como e … gruesomeness," Magda interrupting, "Anyhow, I identify with her bellyjobs and breastjobs and jawjobs and who knows what else … you descend into the trevas … "

"The what?" asks Nona.

"Trevas … the shadows … you descend into the Shadows of the Valley of Death, every surgery's that … and then you vampirically are reborn.

The Phoenix Syndrome. It's not just a question of improving your body/ face, it's like car-racing or parachuting or gliding around with one of those big wings ... and after you're reborn there's the Enemies who have shit on you, you go back to them if they're still (bloated, swollen, sagging, broken, cancerously) alive, and you fly in their windows, 'Remember me?' And they don't, they expect you to have abused life the way they have, but you haven't, you've put it all into the Life Force, your god is Life/Body ... Brockman's got his money and his blood-pressure, Moag's finally turned into a sodden sponge of cirrhotic liver, MacArthur's on top in the NEA like a vulture on the capitol dome ... Anjo da Morte/Angel of Death ... remember BOOM?"

"O que?" asks Bernadette, "What?"

"Movie by Tennessee Williams. Richard Burton and Elizabeth Taylor. Williams knew. He went into the trevas nightly, I saw him, his knockout sleeping pill and then down ... "

"Igh!" shudders Nona, "it's so cold ... " and she pulls the drapes tighter shut.

"Eu entendo o que estão falando," says Bernadette, "I understand what you're talking about. There's lots of people I know that I'd like to fly into the room at the moment of their death ... "

Nona points the heater more directly at them, pulls a blanket around herself.

Long, thin, white fingers reaching up, out, across the green ...


### xviii.

When the article comes out the title reads:

BICHAS, BICHOS E 'KNOW-HOW' ECONOMICA ...

DYKES, BUGS AND ECONOMIC KNOW-HOW ...

And there's a picture of Nona and Magda intertwined out of this old lesbian anthology that Magda's got a copy of in her 'study.' Did someone lift that?

The next day the other Bernadette (boss) tells her, "Oh, there's this woman in town with a collection of lesbian literature ... "

"But why didn't they tell me they had the picture? Dirty journalism ... "

"Don't worry," says Bernadette, "people forget, they forget ... "


### xix.

Bernadette's house was right opposite Margaret's and Alexandra's school, Coração de Jesús.

"Come by and I'll give you cha (tea) and then drive you home ... "

Long house, the active streetworld outside, but then inside, it's a grandfather clock pendulum world, and the handcarved Art Deco dining room furniture, the macramé hangings, the futuristic paintings, are all cancelled out by the measured melancholy of the pendulum.

Picture of Bernadette's mother on the dining-room wall, the TV on (Pica Pau Amarelo), but that doesn't exist either, the mother exists (hovers) in Bernadette pouring out yogurt into little dishes.

"Misturei com manga, mais acho que estava ruin/I mixed it with mangos, but I think they were 'bad' ... "

The kind of thick, white "natural" yogurt you get at Sol da Terra.

Nona tastes it.

"It's OK ... "

"I'm allergic to mangos," says Magda.

Bettina's there too, the juicy one, the replica of the chicken-breasted Italian grandmother, Mediterranea resurgent, but she's cancelled out too, it's true about the slippers, when Papái walks he shuffles, there's a rhythm-tie between slippers and pendulum.

Rhythm-conduit to the past.

"You look just like her, don't you ... " says Magda, fixed on the mother's picture.

"She was bigger," says Bernadette, "she doesn't look bigger there, but she was ... "

Lines at the side of the nose, mouth, eyes, drawn, dragged (down), and there's the long, thin nose, the light in the eyes apagando-se ... going out ... "She just didn't have any lungs left," Bernadette's explained before, "by the time she started to do anything about it she just didn't have any lungs left ... "

Even Magda feels her presence, she's never left, she's there buttering her bread, a little banana-squash jam, coffee with hot (edge-of-boiled) milk, she coughs, the cough's deep, at the same time "shallow," it says it's way, way inside, but there's not much there to be deep inside of ... the father looks startled, worried, all the years of all the kids (poor) and she's been his only friend ... without her, "One, two, three, four, five," says the father in flawless English.

"Great!" says Magda, "wonderful accent."

"Não sei muito, mas o que sei sei bem/I don't know much, but what I know, I know well ... "

No one talks.

Pica-Pau Amarelo, the mother coughing shallowly in the cold, dusty afternoon shadows, and Bernadette there her replica.

"It's like it's all pre-arranged, I'm the surrogate ... my presence keeps the balance the same, which would be OK if I was just replica, but I'm not,

I really can't just be 'extension,'" says Bernadette later.

Out of the shadows, the dark, yoga-lungs, columna vertebral, straining through shells and membranes for that first agonizing, retching gasp of starving air ...


## xx.

Greedy Magda. The money she gets on private-students is HERS. Greedy-guilty. The other (salary) money is "pragmatic" money, food, rent, medicines, children's shoes, but her private-student money is "ego-money," play-money. There's these clear plastic shoes with the red feather puff-balls on the vamp that she's got her eyes on, and she's got this thing about black stockings and tights, the leg's The Thing, and a dress a month, maybe, only there's not that much black around, if she'd only learned how to sew, buys black velvet, Bernadette and Nona make her a skirt, black velvet with a trim of black lace. And Santa Catarineses are small, not so much the Germans in the interior (Blumenau, Joinville), but on the island they're all these runty proto-Mediterranean types, and so size 9-10 shoes (except for the backless plastic ones where your foot can ooze over the sides a bit), forget it, and she starts having them made to order, boots (full-length and ankle-length), high-heeled sandals, she's got this one pair of patent-leather Italian shoes she takes down to the Chilean shoemaker that he duplicates in black suede, straps all over the feet and ankles.

She stands in front of the mirror, in spite of a few bulging vein-spots, these juicy legs.

"Wait'll I lose weight, I'll be dangerous."

But it all takes ego-money, so how can she explain, when it comes time for Bernadette to pay, Magda says "I can't feel right about taking money from you any more."

"But you're tutoring me in English, aren't you?"

"We're talking, right? But you hardly talk any more English anyhow ... "

Smiling, although it's true, she comes in all soft in black harem pants and turban and stretches out on the bed and talks.

São Paulo, her residency in plastic surgery, "There was this one place, things from India, Saris, you can hardly believe the richness, colours, textures, I love fuchsia with gold thread ... and all these coral necklaces, you'd love black coral ... in fact we ought to go back there together, all three of us, my sister, Tereza, lives in São Paulo, married to this high-school teacher who works sixteen hours a day, two full days every day, I don't know how he does it ... "

A different person, really, a family of deep-sea mutes swimming through the dark waters of accumulated socio-religious-political conservatism/repression, and here she is bubbling on, spangle-foam instead of the ominous deep ... and all in Portuguese.

"And besides, that's not the point. I don't know ... voce sabe ... ou não? You know, or don't you?"

"Eu sei ... I know ... "

The little lizard-face all knowing, hard-boiled eggyoke eyes under half-closed lids.

Her little hand up under Magda's poncho, across her nyloned back, pausing at the breasts and then withdrawing ...

### xxi.

Clarice Lispector's *Um Sopro de Vida*, deathbed writing, the writing watching herself dissolve, dissolving on the page, dissolving into clitoral nipples and cicada-rubbing legs, dissolving into god, the divine juice/stew, dissolving into breath.

Teatro Ruth Escobar – Galpão, São Paulo. Marilena Ansaldi's turned the novel into dance-drama, all white, boney, deliciously aging white velvet flesh, nude.

"I've never seen a nude body on stage before," says Magda, retracts, "Folies Bergère ... Julian Beck's Paradise Now, but ... "

Excited.

Beyond pornography into the unified expression of mind as body, body as mind, flesh as thought, thought as flesh.

They all tingle as the flesh pulls tight around the ribs and the thighs contract, although Magda wants to say "There ought to be a little more Lispector and a little less Ansaldi," when they walk out into the metallic-starred cold wind-sheeted Paulistic night and Bernadette says with tragic earnestness, "It's ME, that's what I want," Magda steps back and watches the spirit of Ansaldi possess Bernadette's thin white sexuality.

### xxii.

During the five years since Alexandra's birth, Nona had been unsuccessfully trying to get rid of this huge flabby flap of a belly. Wednesday's Bernadette's yoga-class, and she invites them both along, Magda (hidden – Susannah and the Elders) ashamed/afraid, she's been twenty-two years (her eldest son's age) with a "belly," slowly has honed down food (control) to Point Minimum (psychically bearable), and her face is "good" now, no one ever took her for 47.

But the exercise she did didn't seem to touch the flab, and she longed for a BODY again, especially the tight ribs, Nona's hands around a small waist, heaven was a neat (nitido) instrument of a bed-dance body, and hell was a slob-body incapable of the curved plasticity of love as Death by Candlelight. But when it came time to actually GO, put on the "regulation" turquoise top and beige tights.

"I'll be Babá (Grandmother/babysitter), you guys go ahead … "

And Nona did go, Magda stayed home, but inspired by Bernadette's Faith (Nona asking "Will it really work?" Bernadette nodding in slow yogic affirmation), she spread this big quilted cotton blanket on the floor in the living room and began to work.

The asanas she remembered off the TV in East Lansing, Lilas and You, especially down on all fours like a lion, breathing in, pulling the gut up, or bent over, palms on knees, force all breath out, then pull up/in.

Nona and Bernadette came home all flushed, hot, exhausted.

Coffee ceremony, whole wheat ("brick") bread, butter-honey, Goiaba/Guava, Fig, Quince jellies, all of them in tights, ponchos, sweaters. Magda would say ENTROPY to herself, would say "I'm 47, ten more years and I'll be an old lady," but in the next breath would be saying "It's as if I believe without wanting to, against all logic or even anything I've ever heard of, that I'll pass over somehow, that the body I shape now, my intentions, whole thrust, will be the body I'll pass over with … "

"Pass over?" asks Bernadette, nibbling on a piece of bread smothered in requeijão, the gooey, salty, almost gluey cheese that she loves, especially with fig jam.

"The resurrection of the body, I guess," says Magda, thinking only I can say this in this frozen, medieval Santa Catarina night, island-ship shuddering beyond sea into sky, voyaging in search of god(s).

And the next day again, sitting on the second floor terrace facing the jungle-garden, cold-grey, but there it was below her, the bamboo and the persimmons, palms, eucalyptus, her all wrapped up in tights and wool ponchos, sitting on a wool blanket, she flowed out into the cold, emerald green, but couldn't get rid of Rilke's *schrechlich* angel, hovering around her (Christ promised the kingdoms of this world) promising immortality.


### xxiii.

It seemed like Bernadette's face never changed expression. She'd got frozen, pinched, shrunken, solemnly emotionless, emotionlessly solemn, numb, edge-of angry. She was always thinking, they found that out later, but like Nona would be on the edge of an asthma attack, and Bernadette would seem not to notice, Magda would panic (always bronchitis/asthma, but never before so acute) and afterwards Bernadette would document the Hour, até a hora/even the hour. But you couldn't pick up the "care" and "emotion." Maybe the amusement at words like EAR OF CORN or HOOKS AND EYES, laughing, letting it happen, even little squishes of wrinkles around the corners of the eyes of her wrinkleless mask-face.

And then the clothes began to change, instead of the dichotomy between KALI-TARA, she began to choose intermediate day-states between, nothing white any more, dyeing everything, but not just black, purples, pinks, greens, knit shoes and wrap-around skirts, hair pulled back and tied. A classic Cameo profile.

"Where are your people originally from?" asked Magda. "Milano?"

"Padua ... "

Showed them pictures of her grandmother. Like the grandmother reincarnated. And then one day she actually came home with an announcement.

"I talked to the director of the hospital today, set a 'break-date' for leaving, January the first, and instead of getting angry or anything like that, he said 'Everyone has to work out his own destiny (seu próprio destino) ... ' and everyone else was positive too – which surprised me. Like this one friend of mine said he envies me, he'd like to get out too, only how ... ? He said that no one can be happy in Medicine, all you get is a slanted view of reality, the monster, minority view, reality as twisted, never the majority all's well-that-functions-well view ... "

"But you'll do me before you finish," worries Magda about the face-lift she's started to obsess over.

"After Christmas. Do you want to fix a date right now?" Taking out her appointment book. "The twenty-seventh, how's that?"

"OK. And why the sour-puss?"

"Sour ... ?"

"Cara feia. Why the cara feia with me? You don't want to do it, do you?"

"No."

The little face tightens up, reverts back, back, back, back ... small little bedrooms, there's nine of you, but the image is sitting on the floor in an Alice in Wonderland dress staring at a broken doll, the other eight invisibly absent.

"Why not?"

"Do I have to tell you?" Nona knitting in, "It's hard enough to cut strangers, she loves you, you cluck ... "

Striking Magda as strange, that anyone could/should love her, the word 'love' strange, as if there were nothing to love, her imploded vacuum emptiness. In each other's arms, Bernadette was so small, you never thought of her as that small until she was bonily diminutive in your arms.

"It's not that I want it either (looking for a splinter of a mirror, confirmation of existence), but ... "

The Dark invades the sun-room, all of a sudden Frank Sullivan's there. When they finally opened him up he was filled with tumours, all over his stomach, up and down his spinal cord.

And her favourite Dead begin to fill the room, Errol Flynn and Virginia Woolf, Aldous Huxley and Emily Brontë and Gustav Mahler, Keats and Samuel Barber, Sylvia Beach and Zelda Fitzgerald ...

Which is a pure lie, isn't it, to invoke them out of the Emptiness, when that's all they are now ... Emptiness ...

"I just think that ... when I did that book, *Letters of an Old Pro*, I read literally hundreds of autobiographies of 'stars,' and there's this tenacity ... Dietrich, Gloria Swanson ... you hang on with your claws ... the purpose of medicine isn't survival but triumph. As long as you possibly, possibly can ... it's a commitment to juiciness ... Neo-Epicureanism. Either I believe it and act on that belief, or ... "

Sullivan's going down, the big Notre Dame fullback, he's lying down now, Deathmask and Dusk and the Peace that Accompanies the End of Understanding.


### xxiv

The whole colegiado/department in the room (Carmen Rosa, Bygate, Derrick, Hilario, Magda, Mike Jayne), Jayne gets up and locks the door.

"You don't mind, do you?" Madga bites her lips, Mike Monkeyface turns the key, sits back down. "The reason I want to lock things up a bit is Vanya. I'm rather disturbed about her overall performance-level ... "

"Especially considering the fact that it was you who bulldozed her into the programme in the first place," says Carmen Rosa.

Mike smiling a wide, insolent grin at her.

"Be that as it may, I think she should be 'discontinued' from the programme ... "

"And how do you propose to 'discontinue' her?" asks Englishman Bygate, amused, always amused by the Americans.

"Well, nothing drastic, in fact rather painlessly," said Mike, "we simply all give her C's ... "

"But we're at mid-term, she hasn't handed in any work yet," says Magda.

"That's not the point," says Mike, "the point is that her overall performance isn't up to par ... "

"Well, I think that's a fairly objective evaluation," says Hilario, and Magda clamps up/acids up, walks out in a silent flurry of protest, the Santa Catarina Island day outside like Irish summer. She loves the long grass palm-dune days. She wants to be out where she was the first days on the island, on the dunes, damn the snakes (which everyone talked about but which she never saw) out by Lagoa, walking to São Jaoquina, a whole universe isolated inside the hot isolated dune-hollows, smelling the (winter) sea as you walk toward it, birds barraging down around you, The Intruder, in a lost-world where no one intrudes, in the Sambaqui-world of her imagination, before the slaughter of the Indians, slaughter of Paradise, slaughter of … Vanya. When Harry Smith had been down the year before (Christmas), Vanya's sister, Vera, had had them out to their beachhouse (where they lived all year around) at Campeche, this huge churrasco/barbecue, Vera supplying the salads and trimmings, Magda the meat, and they'd gone down to this roughest beach on the island and got lost in the violet sky-sea. Vanya was big-breasted, a transplanted Dago-beauty, the Soul of Sadia/Sane. This funny-strong Italian accent, but the Portuguese (and English) were coming along.

All full of zest, inner energy.

And now they all (Star Chamber) seemed to agree – Vanya was dead. And on to the next order of business – bringing down Leslie Fielder, another one of Jayne's obsessions. Not that Magda had anything against Fielder, but Jayne – a 45-year-old ex-Weatherman turned KKK-ish in Brazil as a last ditch stand to stay in the profession – Jayne she had everything against, had never met anyone who so incarnated the hard-boned, abusive, insensitive, punishing spirit of The Stag. Walking out into the corridor first, the others (as always) lingering on sucking on and loving their officialese, fifteen, twenty minutes more of flattering, patting each other, Carmen Rosa, that whore, puxa-saco/pull-bag, scrotum-tickling … but they all fell for it, didn't they?

Magda fingernail-flipped her hair over her forehead, thought "Slavic," this massive, heavy, marble clunk of a forehead, and her thin, greying, slavic hair. She ought to dye it blonde, blonde afro, give it some body.

And then later Vanya in Magda's office.

"So, what did they decide?"

"What do you mean?"

"Jayne said that today was my day, final jugamento … "

"Judgement. So he said something to you beforehand?"

"In class yesterday he said that the students were organizing against him and that I was behind the whole thing. Which I'm not, honestly, I'm not. In fact no one's really organizing against him. They just don't want him to turn two hours into four hours, adicionar, como é … ?"

"Add … "

"Add all kinds of extra written work, insist on a final exam when all along he said he wasn't going to have one."

"Well ... " Magda holding in, crossbow-tense, and then suddenly shooting into the heart, letting it go, "You're getting flunked out of the programme ... "

"But how, I haven't handed in any work yet ... "

"Well, that's a good question. I'll tell you, the leader of the rebellion is Jandyra, if there really is a leader and if there really is a rebellion. Maybe it's more accurate to say that the strongest woman in the class is Jandyra, and she's had it with Jayne's fanaticism. You know, she's fed up with his full-time Big Professor Ego-Trip. Only he can't fight her back, so he needs a scapegoat ... "

"Como?"

"Bode expiatório ... and that's you ... "

"Only you're not going to flunk me ... ?"

"I don't have to, all I'm supposed to do is give you a C. Everyone gives you C's and you're dead ... "

"But you're not going to give me a C, are you?"

"When I see your papers ... "

And then the pack-ice breaks, tortured Past and iffy Future all suddenly erupting out into a cancerous Now.

"It's only a grade for you, but for me it's life, give me an A, I'll do anything for you, you know I'm a brilliant student, I only need a chance to prove myself. I've never been able to travel like the others, they've had years, some of them, in the US, I've never left Brazil ... "

"Don't worry, for me tudo bem/everything's fine," says Magda, hating to see such Beauty reduced to THIS. Reduced TO BY ...

She holds Vanya close up against her, holds her and holds her and holds her and she cries and cries and cries.

Until The Englishman sticks his nose in, humorously sniping, "I'm not interrupting anything am I?"

"Fee, Fi, Fo, Fum, as a matter of fact, you are ... "

"I'll come back ... "

And he's gone.

Magda's mind slowly tumbling Vanya down on the violet sand, manta ray mouth between her legs, gasping, her Buddha-voice whispering "Your nipples are the lotuses of wisdom, your cunt the portal to beatitude, the enemy is Head, Head is Hell, forget it and become the vibrations of Pure Paradiso ... "

Only ("All I want is a chance to prove myself!") she knows that Vanya's gone, lost, off the sense-hook, sinking into the vast engulfment of the abstract male sea ...

That night Hilario calls her up, with his careful cupboard priest-voice (touch of venom – why did he ever leave the priesthood?)

"I hear you're going to give Vanya an A. You can't do that you know, we all agreed to give her a C ... "

Magda suddenly back waitressing, car-washing, hustling around in hard summer-street Chicago.

"I wish she'd kill herself and leave a note with your name on it as the person who drove her to it. If she could only die without dying. You have no sensitivity, no sense of justice, rules, procedures. You'll be the first one to condemn the military for violating habeas corpus, but ... "

She stops, suddenly contracts, folds, holds in, hangs up.

Canalha/Shithead!

To violate the peace of my Lotus World.

"Who's that?" asks Nona, Magda trying to not let The Madness invade the calm. Only it's there now, guilt, uncertainty, the fucker's there, anger, loss of control against the eternal Father, Father, Son and ...

I'm the Holy Spirit, she thinks, as she goes into Nona to confess all.


### XXV.

Madga and Bernadette on the bed in the Black Topaze Chamber, Chacrina's Discoteca on the TV, Chacrina dressed as bride, seventy-year old pot-bellied dirty old clown.

The discotheque girls, all twenty of them, juicily, if too athletically, dressed in tennis shoes and lycra exercise suits that show up the sweat-spots under their breasts and on their bellies.

"What a waste of beautiful women," says Magda, "it's so goofy, on Tuesday nights, when they have Amateur Hour (Calouros), the girls are all in these high-heeled boots, I mean they're really gorgeous women. But lycra gym-suits ... only even in their gym-suits they're all so 'parabolic,' that's what they're chosen for, vulgar/vulgate bodies ... "

Lilian comes on, English (?) in this mesh body-glove and black boots, the song's irrelevant, the pumping mesh thighs are everything, camera shots dwell on thighs and breasts, eyes orgasming with the camera, quick, short shots back and forth between the singer and the girls, shots of the audience, these hundreds of empty-headed sound-drowned teenage faces, mouthing, bouncing, bobbing along, back to Lilian, black-mesh bones. Madga herself, as always, in black tights and lycra-top, shots of gigantic bananas hanging from the ceiling, shots of swinging arses, below-behind. Bernadette unmade-up, this brown acetate shirt on, cotton top. Nona's in putting the kids to bed. She believes in bedding down (contact) with them, the door's open, outside, beyond the screened and shuttered window, spring winds are rattling through the vinyl-sounding palms.

Bernadette's caressing Magda's left leg, foot, Magda's just taken a little Guaraná and honey, her nipples tingle.

"I love the feel of acetate."

Bernadette leans back, hair between Magda's legs, Magda's hands, palms open, crest across the tips of Bernadette's breasts, Magda mouths down over Bernadette's mouth, Bernadette sucks on Magda's tongue, Magda's hand up between her legs. She's got these black lace panties on.

"Disguise," says Magda, pulling them down, fingers carefully reaching for the swollen clitoral bulb, Bernadette biting Magda's lips.

There's this one girl Chacrinha calls Panterinha/Little Panther, who steps out of the ranks and weaves around black-net Lilian, as Bernadette's mouth descends between Magda's thighs.

Sirens, bells, foghorns, they re-pattern on the bed, like scorpions, and it all becomes acrid, coppery salty tastes and sudden butterfly-heart spasmings, muscles like steel wires, a variety of small hurt/ecstatic cries … as Lilian finishes and there's a sudden switch to the Detefon commercial. There's this bug in a tux, tights and long thin black shoes that comes out and Chacrina goes after him with this huge fake spraycan of Detefon and sprays out this flocculent plastic spray, as the cries come from deep inside Bernadette, cries of long-waiting hunger and hurt. Magda worries about Nona – this wasn't in the cards.

Implied, maybe, but projected out into some distant, future Michigan rendezvous.

Magda whimpering too as the bug dies, feet up in the air, and is dragged off stage.

"I love you," says Bernadette in this heavy, almost Russian-accented English.

"I love you too," answers Magda.

"E agora os meus amigos, o rei da juventude Brasiliera/And now, my friends, the king of Brazilian youth!"

And this skinny guy in satin trousers and a T-shirt and a sailor hat perched on top of his head, comes out dancing around singing

PIFF-PAFF
PING-PONG
BURACO
CHADREZ …

"Ping-pong, hole, chess?" wonders Magda, as they sit up, their tastes and smell strong on their mouths and hands.

For a long time Nona has been encouraging Bernadette to move in, leave Medicine, leave home, work the whole madness and magic here even within this, her world.

Later that night, over corn-bread and coffee, Bernadette says "Maybe I will move in … " And later she explains the lyric. "It's four kinds of games, two card-games, Piff-Paff and Buraco and Ping Pong and Chess/Chadrez … "


## xxvi.

It was a Sunday afternoon wasn't it, the girls were outside playing with Katia and Simone, after lunch, lying on the burgundy satin sheets in the ecru-glow of light bouncing through the thin slits of the shutters.

Cansaço/Fatigue.

Descending drugged and grinning with barely-opened Arabian-afternoon black orgiastic eyes, the moment of stick, stuck, dissolve, Magda in the middle, arms under their heads, then her legs draped over theirs like she's crucified, like a crab/spider flipped over on its back.

The heater's on, Sonia's brother, Sergio, wooded over all the cracks around the windows (the day he stole all the tools) so the heat stays in, they're at the perfect point of balance/ease, neither moving in nor out, adjusting in or out, covering or uncovering, just right, toastily-cold.

Bernadette's said a while back something about "touching."

There was this Chilean Bio-Dance group, finger-tip to finger-tip, sensitization to The Other (Je suis Autre), you respond/interrelate-act on the level of micro-awareness (Nous Sommes Autres).

Nona's hand first bloodclaws over black dance-thighs, down to the Centre, Magda in her decaying Persian-melon juiciness, Ohs, slits in her tights, "mucosal liberation," she has masturbated a lot, that keeps coming out, "I think it's especially the fate of the only child, you create an Autre because, if you didn't … if I may use the terms, the Wound of Loneliness would never heal … "

Hand through black mesh panties, trying to go under the mesh.

"No, leave it there."

The Theory of Transferred, Layered, Veiled Stimulus. Magda's hands begin to weave delicate patterns around the peaks of breasts, bite hair, dragon-tongues lick necks.

"You're so non-salty in winter … "

Door closed, the children's voices outside.

"I worry about the effect of all this on them," Nona says a lot.

Distant mosquitos on the other side of night-screens, the room becomes lungs, throats, eyes close or slit open to glimpse a black foot, red nails, Bernadette of the enormous nipples, the athletic starved body, and Nona's flab slowly moulding into precise (limão verde/green lime) flesh.

"Someone, my breasts!" and Bernadette reaches up under black lycra and starts to fingertip as Magda's hands snake down between their thighs. The picture is black wool whirlpool waves out of which emerge open red mouths, tongues, teeth, brown-pink nipples, pink, thigh-bounded mouths.

The picture is Massacre.

Form becomes cry, colour becomes clotted by the black threads of agonizing, high shrill trumpets. The Ronscevalle canyons are wide and vast, the three voices keen shrill brass with lion-metal canyon-bottom tones that last and last and last, then finally stop … as the Daystar obliques blinds through the children's voices again, all toasty-warm …


### xxvii.

Magda listening, wondering how Maureen had got where she was (on the balcony of Polly's over nice steaks, bacon-fried farofa, French Fries, a chicken-potato salad (cold) mayonnaise, the first Advent orchids blooming in the trees in Praça XV), tiny and puffy and red and very Scotch-Irish with this broad Midlands (Leeds) accent, and hair like an unwashed, uncombed, uncut caramel-coloured poodle.

"We went down to his place at Pantanal do Sul, dropped acid, this most beautiful sunset, it was just so neat … transcendental … you know what I mean, transcendental?"

"What about Carmen?" asks Magda.

"I don't know," says Maureen, this puffy wrinkled elf giggle, "What about her?"

"Do you like her?" asks Nona, "I mean, have you met her?"

"I've met her. She's all right. Maybe a bit of a Dodo. Literally. Wingless extinction. But Paulo has a kind of filial fondness for her, so I tolerate the old cow, buy her presents. I suppose it's the closest I've ever come to actually kissing arse. But he's worth it, and that place by the beach. I've never seen such a sky … "

"Where do we go from here?" asks Nona, nibbling away at a cold French fry left over on her plate, Margaret and Alexandra up now, bored, leaning over the balcony, looking down at the crowds, Magda always calling them back over, 'Don't lean over the edge,' the vision always of poor construction inside the wood-covering, and them falling before their time.

"Well, I'm going back to São Paulo to do another Awareness Workshop. John's kind of 'softening' the group for me now. I come in and give them the final wallop. That's three thousand for the week. And then on to Rio. And maybe after that back here. There's so much interest in sociosexuality in Brazil these days, it's kind of Mass Horniness. All the Luso-Catholic Puritanism is going by the bye, bye, bye. Well (she looks around, she's eaten her Admiral's share of meat and potatoes, you wonder how she stays as wrinkled-runty as she is), I'd better be on my merry. I'm supposed to meet Paulo at three. If we could just duplicate our last acid-love performance … " she's up, checking in her purse, "Oh, I left my money with Paulo, you wouldn't mind picking up the tab, would you? I'll pay you later … "

"No problem," says Nona, Magda just looks.

"Look at the orchids," says Maureen as Nona writes out a cheque, "Ah, Brazil, Brazil, oh meu Brasil … how did you get so bloody horny?"

Later at Carmen's-Bernadette's office, Nona's got this wart growing out all over her thumb, and Carmen's nitric-aciding it. Not that it's working. Bernadette's talking about taking off the nail altogether if the thing grows up, under.

"We had lunch with Maureen today," says Magda, "the penniless little rich girl."

"Oh, she's always bringing me presents, but who does she think she's kidding? Meu deus do céu/God in Heaven!"

The poor girl from the backwoods mountain fazenda/ranch in Minas, every time Magda looks at her she hears her saying (after her last visit home) "It's such a shock to go back after ten years, you leave people vigorous and come back to them almost 'gone.'"

"What I can't understand," says Magda, "is how anyone can want to put it in her … "


### xxviii.

Bernadette kissing Magda "afterwords."

"Que cheiro tão gostoso/What a delicious smell … "

"E de voce/it's you," answered Magda.

No, she's never "given" the way she gives Bernadette, she goes right to "detestable" kidneys, heart, liver, that's where the only "flavour" is.

The taste of rivers … opening …

Bethlehem/Belém and the desembocadura of the delicious muddy shit Amazonas, your eyes, mouth, nose gets lost in the gusto of cranes rising up from the lost ceramic world of Marajó.


### xxix.

No paved road to the south of the island, Pantano do Sul. So it remained unbourgeoised, untouristed, almost, almost the way it had been five thousand years before – except for the intrusion of a few fishermen who'd been there for a couple of hundred years.

A church on a bay. Self-sufficiency. Açorianos, the vanguard of Portuguese colonial operations.

Sand, roads through dunes, past forests. Magda was sure they were going to get stuck.

"I wish it would rain. It's easier when it's wet," said Bernadette, but she barrelled, bounced, barraged on until there they were on a hill overlooking this wide sweep of a bay, rocky backboned heaps of mountains that stuck dramatically out into the water.

Grey day, clouds, on the edge of rain.

"I love it," said Magda, "it reminds me of Land's End, Ireland, the furthest west point of land in Europe. Before you hit the Americas. Green, all those backbones of mountains and the sudden drop down to the sea. Even the smell, jeito/essence, the clouds on the edge of mist … "

Thinking Machu Picchu, how she'd wanted to dissolve there, the non-tourist-filled day all alone watching the clouds born below her in the Urubamba Valley.

Death as Cosmic Orgasm.

"We have to walk from here," said Bernadette, parking the car behind a fishing-boat shack, fisherman on the beach, more out in the water.

"Where's the house?" asks Nona.

"Out there … " pointing to almost the end of the left landjut, "that little yellow house with the tile roof … "

A touch of wet in the air.

"I love it," says Magda, passing down to/through the beach, cumbersome fishing boat beached, the catch all over the sand, a manta-ray turned over on its back, its mouth gasping for air, a mouth without eyes or nose, desperate, the cut-off tail stump bleeding into the sand.

"Mãe/Mum," says Margaret, and the girls clutch up against Nona.

"Sangue/blood," says innocent Alexandra, the well-shaft to the depths of innocence.

"Algunes são muitos lindos/Some are very pretty," says Bernadette, running her hand-eye over the body of the long wet-silver, fleshy-silverfoil, needle-toothed fish, the fishermen all small, runty, hardly noticing them, tourists (auslanders) versus Work.

The ray-mouth still screaming for air.

"It makes me afraid," says Magda as they move on, off the sand up onto the rocky path, there's sea, path, tobacco-road ancient poverty houses, the smell of shit, then a space, a cemetery.

"It's beautiful," says Nona, white crosses and the green grass facing on the cold green-white sea.

"I'd like to be buried here. Imagine the pilgrimages of my 'fans,' make the trip worthwhile even without me inside … "

Magda unable to shake the idea that she'd always be where she was buried, always BE, period, linger on dissolving into a consciousness called sea, mist, land, cemetery, dirt … lama as in High Parvati-Lama.

The mist, waves, the "Dead" all looking at them, "infiltrating," invading, sucking at, longing for them to be part of Them, no single digits, compartments, only conglomerates, wholes, animate, inanimate.

No more houses now, just path and rock extending out into the sea in broad, black sheets, like massive black beards.

"It's just up there … " Carmen waiting for them.

"I thought you got lost … "

"Not yet," says Magda, "but it'd be a good place to start now."

Fresh whole wheat and corn bread so puffily granular that you can hardly cut it into slices, a pitcher of fresh milk, fresh coffee, jellied guave, banana-squash (with a touch of cinnamon) jam, heavy white-yellow pear-honey, a crock of fresh butter, a pitcher of plain yoghurt spumed with fresh mangos and honey, crackers, a crumbling honey-soggy banana-laced cake.

"When we bought it it was just a fishing shack (casabre), really … or let's not be too hard on it … house (casa) … the roof's the same, the walls … we just added bathrooms … "

"There was this mountain of merde/shit out in the garden," says Bernadette.

"Don't even talk about it," Carmen mock-retches.

White walls, the underbelly of the russet tiles just placed on wood rafters, built in benches covered with huge puffball pillows ranged all around the walls, a shark's jaws hanging, a dried snake …

"In the summer we all used to come out here. We'd be all over the floors. There's these built-in hooks for hammocks … "

"How is Paulo?" asks Magda. No such things as taboos are there? Magda looking out through the window, white semen foam on the blackboard Orocks, How could Man (generic) ever be so greedy as to expect Heaven too … ?

"He's in São Paulo with Maureen and John, I guess. They're liable to get into a car and drive off to Maranhão … who knows … "

"And you?" asks Nona.

"Well … "

She shakes her shaggy lionness head, not in infinite sadness but a small dampness, crumbling, loosening, weakening of fibre.

"And you wonder why you feel the way you do about yourself … " says Magda.

"I don't know … " Carmen pinching, prodding into her belly, pulling up around her eyes, "You want to do a face-lift (uma plastica) on me too?"

"Acho que não precisa, I don't think you need it," says Bernadette, "another five or ten years."

"I think you're a beautiful woman," says Magda.

"You really are," agrees Margaret, her mouth full of cake, milk, butter, honey. Alexandra all eyes/interest, but eating's a serious no-talk ceremony for her, especially the mango-pulped yoghurt.

They fill themselves up with split, curly, expanded, puffy bread, smear it all over with honey and butter and fruit-jams, wash it all down with milk and coffee.

It's cozy inside, even outside. Later there's a Presence of behind-clouds sun. They bring blankets out, stretch out on the grass.

"No danger of snakes?" asks Magda.

Carmen shakes her head, Bernadette spunky-punky, "You should have seen this place when Carmen first bought it. I mean apart from the pile of merde … everything rocky, uneven … empty … we planted all the palms, the persimmons … "

"There was some bamboo … "

Stretched out framed in the surrealistically exaggerated largeness of leaves, limbs, fruit, the air, light bright with moisture on the edge of mist, no sound except for the kids playing, the surf, the wind through the leaves, bamboo …

"If you expect heaven too, it's almost greedy," says Magda.

"I even forget to remember what's wrong," laughs Carmen, Magda a Pietá in Nona's arms, Magda's arms loose around Bernadette's legs, Carmen watching, a little distant (outside) like a curious Centurion … as the sun-cithra plays with long afternoon fingers beyond the cover of the clouds.


**XXX.**

Magda in her room alone, the Spirit descends on her, coals in a grate all jiggled afire, one last pair of the rarest garments in the world, black support stockings (that grip the legs like clamps of black steel) and then this black stretch-lace corset with the nipples she's artfully cut out, and Bernadette's crocheted around so that the emerging cork-tip nipple is the centre of a black rose, another black rose at the centre of the cut out crotch, high-heeled black suede boots with (again Bernadette) fake emeralds sewed into the vamp, black lace collante (leotard) top and black lace skirt, then a careful whitening of the face, black eyes and lips so they'll hang etched/

suspended in the Christmas red nightlight when Bernadette (her night) comes in and turns off the overhead light.

Nona is in bed with the kids, Bernadette still in the bathroom. Magda can hear her puttering around, lights a red candle, stretches out on the black satin sheets, looks at herself in a small hand-mirror, the shameless jaguarish eye-lines working, suspended in the ashamed blushlight. Thinking Mae West on the afternoon TV, old cowgirl film, round face, fat, later with the surgery she got so angular, her skin sandpapery, corrosive.

I oughta have my belly operated on at the same time I have my face done, I don't really believe in yoga … massage …

Thinking about Hildegard Nef's account of Dietrich, old lady Hitler-neurotic, MA VIE EN ROSE, until The Fall, and then … Remembering her meeting with Leslie Caron in the Tate in London, the awful etch-(cut-) lines around the sad dog eyes, and then Valentino Nazimova never looked that "drawn," as if they know the lie, even if the surface knows better, Betty Grable just before she died so unwrinkled, puffed full of life, hunchback cancer deform-corroding through her breasts, and who'd even recognize summer stock Hedy Lamarr as Ecstasy … ? The door opens and Bernadette comes in, all black chiffon, shivering, then expanding out into the orange-electric-coiled heat.

"Tão quentinho aca … "

And she comes to the bed, ten years younger than when she first met her, the pinched, old-maidish, starved runty apprehensiveness replaced by uptilted almost-fleshy face-as-shield/ice-cutter/singing axe, not just "accepting," but welcoming this reality.

"Tudo bem?/Everything OK?"

And tongues touch (carefully), you mustn't disturb the (careful) outlines of the sacred lipstick. As legs begin to rub together, she loves the strained pneumaticness of the stockings, tongue as lance moving down between the legs. She likes to be grasped, held pressed, she likes to writhe, be trapped and spitted, scourged and crucified, suddenly feels this Heraclitean-fire orgasm wild-fire through her. Christ as female, breasts and black (support) stockings …

"Even if it was only tonight, only now … "

"Como … ?" asks Bernadette.

"Nada/Nothing … apois/later … "

Then afterwards, dawn is brittly ice-edging across the sky, Magda time to time reassuring herself in the wall-mirror that she is.

"I've spent so much of my life in libraries, at desks typing, I was beginning to 'break' Mayan hieroglyphics, make Whorf look silly. I could go into a Maya city and feel at home. I knew all the statues within a comfortable Southeast-Asian-Amerindian analogue-context … and there were always the kids, and I believed – that's the word – in the literal sanctity of cooking and bread-making, the biblical good wife/woman, the only things I didn't do were to keep night-watch, make candles and weave. And, you know, you snack a little, your body's not a lethal love-object/weapon, it's a pin-cushion, upholstered armchair, shopping bag, pillow … it becomes Aristotelian passive … "

"Aris … what?"

"Aristotle has the Male as the Active and the Female as the Passive Principles. If western so-called culture had been nursed on Minoan milk instead of Greek semen it would have all been breast-womb upholstered instead of prick-spear centred … Heidegger's right, it does all go wrong with the Greeks, and death-awareness is death-awareness … let's go and shut the gate … "

If they don't Donna Betty's chickens come in and claw in the grass outside the bedroom window, cluck-answer Donna Sylvana's rooster's crowing, the cats come in anyhow, and the spiders and monster roaches. Even when it's down to forty, it's still tropical.

Semen-cloud-seedy bluing sky, the black nightladies shutting out the macho dawn.


### xxxi.

Magda had been toying with the idea of a third year on the island.

Hardly cared what there wasn't, the rain comes, the sun yoke cracks out of the cloud-shells of the afternoon sky, the tropical emerald green stays jade-cold, you sit on the second floor back terrace facing the jungle and it's the same cold-wind San Francisco clear-sun that used to trigger her off into despair-joy just with the presence of the scalpelled cauterising light.

She thinks "Michigan" and it's all dead grey again, you can't even be Body, all you can do is retract, protect against the punishing cold. Cold grey little day-life pellets, look at the grey stairway, the grey 1908 dining room with the old handmade oak table and chairs (contracted, bottled).

And then she opens her eyes and the undersea green richness swims around her.

"The tropics can be God," she tells Bernadette, "people didn't have Chagas when the Europeans first came, it was in the animals like the Tatú but they were so adapted to it that it didn't make any difference. And it was the African slaves that brought the liver flukes. When the Europeans first got here they had this vision of the hundred and fifty year old perfect-health Indian in a perfect astrologically-balanced world … "

Michigan snow, slush, dripping, and then the sudden rush of hot, inland summer as if the Great Lakes were dead, dry, inland seas ...

"We've got a verbal acceptance from Mike Jayne to come back down in March," says Hilario at this meeting just before Christmas, "I just talked to him on the phone yesterday. Now it's just a question of letter-acceptance."

Magda having a hard time believing she's hearing what she's hearing.

"But he just left, got up and walked out."

"You know damned well he had family problems," says Derrick sneeringly.

Magda's tried to make friends with him, "I'm available for invitations," and "Why don't you come over to the house this Sunday, we're having a little churrasco/barbecue for some students, and ... "

Only he'd just give out with those almost-closed-eyes smiles, suck on his pipe, superior, the Berkeley Ph.D. way of saying "Fuck off, don't bug me."

"Who says he won't have them again ... he's such a psychopath," says Magda.

"That's the pot calling the kettle black isn't it?" Derrick answers.

And Magda's hurt. Unexpected. Uncalled for. Examination of conscience. She puts herself placidly next to frenetic Jayne, image of Sweatman steaming down the angry halls, but her "personal" life is, at best, "original." And then all of a sudden she's back in 1968 Puritan Michigan again, she meets Nona, they're both married, but that all evaporates, they move in together, there's the smell of cauterised meat in the air, but indifference takes over, people accept, or – more accurately – don't give a damn.

"Jayne's basically a paranoid-sadist, and I don't think that any man who's done what he's done to a student – Vanya – should be given a second chance ... "

"You know I get so tired of Sapphic witch-trials," says Derrick, and Magda gets up, leaves, hears Hilario asking Derrick, "Tired of what?"

Jandyra. Her husband's a reporter on *Veja*, Brazil's *Time*. She looks like a Hindu, acts like a two-generation-back NYC Jewish mother.

When the word gets to her that Mike's coming back, she's over to Magda's place with "We've got to do something ... " Magda has this Memo that's come out of the meeting that she walked out of, with a list of all the goodies Jayne's had offered to him:

1. Air fare
2. Money to bring down all his books
3. Guaranteed three-year contract
4. Permanent visa

"Jesus!" says Jandyra, "there's no limit, huh ... ?"

Mike's face grinning in the room, "After I'm gone I hope you suffer with Jandyra the way I did … "

"What I think," says Anita this other (55-year-old American baby-doll widow, married to a Brazilian who committed suicide two years before, 25 years in Brazil) grad student, pipes up with "I think Jandyra's idea of bringing it to the newspapers is the only way to get anything done, because Hilario's completely insensitive to student feelings. I mean you've got a genuine full-fledged sadist involved, and for Hilario and Derrick it's all just part of male-bonding."

"Yeah, this 'male-bonding,' what is that anyhow?" says Jandyra, "but under-the-surface dishonest homosexuality … ?"

And they go to the *Jornal da Semana*. Jandyra's husband's a friend of the reporter-poet who's always wanted to meet Jandyra's husband anyhow, and … the article comes out:

PSYCHOPATHIC AMERICAN PROFESSOR GIVEN
PREFERENTIAL HIRING TREATMENT.
With all the details.

Another meeting, Hilario calling her at home, insisting she come. Derrick explodes.

"I wanna know who's behind this (looking at Magda) and have them thrown out," Magda nonplussed, staring him down.

"The picture that comes into mind is a witch-trial in Salem. It's a big joke nowadays, but … "

"It was a canalha/shitty thing to do," says Hilario.

"Well, you don't listen to anyone either," says Magda, "Now you're afraid for your job and the whole thing going public and it's a different matter."

"You and your special connection to the *Jornal da Semana* … " says Derrick.

"That article that came out about me was a slam."

"You loved it," says Derrick, his face all Germanic now, the eyes behind the surgical steel-rimmed glasses, his pipe a horn, all ready to gore Magda.

"I didn't love it," says Magda, Bernadette's fine-tipped fingers/tongue star-wars descent-attacking into her groin, she allows herself to plateau, groan, no shame in the Black Topaze Chamber where you're allowed to animal, to god … and the whole room and all the men (male-bonding) … there's this moment of intense light, and then they shred, fibre, slough off, running into pads, down liquid thaw-drains … And that night the Come is sluggish, she can't seem to get inside the Chamber, part of her stays out in the banana-leaf-rustling wind.

"You ought to see your face," says Nona.

In the red candleglow loving Nona's reddish-pink hair and delicately mascara'd eyes. She begins with dark brown-purple (café) lipstick, but after a few minutes that's rubbed off and all that's left are the startled black eyes painted on a sandface.

"What do you mean?" asks Magda.

"These tiny little angst-angles, your eyebrows tilting up in the middle, this massive Slavic look. Is it the meeting?"

"Really, I want to keep out of things, I should have played diarrhoea again. I don't want it to come in here, but it's like part of me can't make it inside. I'm not air anymore, I've started to petrify and can't make it through the screen … "

"Can you pinpoint it?"

"Well, mainly it's disbelieving me when I say I don't want to go public about our sex life … you know … "

Under all the massive Slavic toughness this little girl in the white muslin dress (Cicero, 1937) who doesn't want to climb up in Mrs Seidel's cherry-tree because she doesn't want to dirty/tear her dress, and doesn't want to show her legs/between her legs to anyone standing down below looking up.

"I know, you put on this thick-skinned 'act,' but that's all it is … "

"And then, just the 'contact' with 'them.' It rubs off, you feel dirty, this fascist inside Derrick. Crusade, cause … they're not close enough to their pricks and balls, really. Sometimes I think that all the aggression-games in the world come from unfulfilled male homosexuality."

"See … " Nona touching Magda between the eyes, it's gone," Magda closing her eyes for a moment, the surface inside the pleasure-dome unstirred, dead, black mirror.

Then looking in the mirror on the dresser, the face frozen, 'startled,' curious, exploratory, anticipatory, very, very young, all of it ahead, to come, mystery.

The other Bernadette (boss) over for lunch, the question of a third year settled (No!) Bernadette has to get out (after Medicine) start new, fresh, elsewhere, there's Nona's mother, Magda's publishing 'contacts,' but Magda's 'fishing,' 'playing.'

"If I wanted to stay another year … "

"Fine with me, but there'd be problems from the grad faculty."

"Derrick … ?"

"Well … "

She doesn't want to say it, Spring is ycumin in, it's such a nice cheese-chicken casserole.

But Magda feels her cells begin to turn to stone, no question about it. The Screens of Night will keep her out, the Black Topaze Chamber demands complete dream, and she finds the passage to sleep blocked by the withhold-frustration madness of the part of her Ph.D.-mind that's male-bonded to 'them.'

Purification, the Descent of Holy Mother Pentecostal FLAME ...


### xxxii.

"No, I get worried," says Elizete.

Twenty-three, but she could be thirty-three, forty-three. Elegantly boney.

And she's got (Jersey, lycra, the good "drapers") style, this necklace of shiny black beads.

"Is that onyx?" asks Magda and Elizete takes it off, Nona reaches out for it.

"It was my grandmother's."

"It's onyx," says Nona, both she and Bernadette not just looking at a piece of jewellery any more, but two technicians looking at technique.

"All the rhomboids and circles. It looks Cretan, Jerichoian, at the same time Victorian. Of course there's these imperial echoes in the Victorian," says Magda.

"How much would it be worth?" asks Elizete.

"A lot," says Bernadette, "you ought to bring lots of jewellery with you to Canada. There's only one way they can go ... up ... "

"Or gold," says Luiz, "there's this ad in *Veja* every month, you buy these little ounce cubes ... "

Nervous, twittery, racoon-eyed Luiz. Magda imagines he has to be great in engineering, but in English nao tem jeito/no talent. A required 500 on the TOEFL/ Test of English as a Foreign Language, and the last time he took it he got ...

"You do look like Bernadette," says Nona, "only it's a little hard to imagine with all that beard, the same eyes ... "

"And if he doesn't get 500 on the TOEFL this time?" asks Elizete, "do you really think we should go up before he passes ... ?"

"I don't know, I just keep thinking of you there in this black, grey, brown, white frozen world. Most of the winter mainly white. Not a touch of green," says Magda.

"I keep worrying about Bernadette, the whole family's worried about Bernadette ... "

Luiz impatient.

"She's 31, for god's sake ... the Brazilian family nodule ... let her alone ... "

"No one understands why you're leaving Medicine," says Elizete.

"You tell me, I don't know," says Bernadette, "será que de veras estou deixando atrás tudo/Could it be that I'm really leaving everything behind?"

"I don't think," says Magda, "that … put it this way, instead of adopting the professions to the reality of woman, woman has to adapt herself to the (male) realities of the profession. Which means a kind of … like stripping down bamboo, you're allowed stalk, but no leaves. OK, you just graduated as an electrical engineer, fine, but if you started on the M.S. and Ph.D. now like Luiz, if it was your TOEFL instead of his, you and the baby and the career … so women, you know, adapt child-raising to the male career-world, adapt their breasts, milk and their menstruations, everything to the time-clock … " Magda stops, looks at Bernadette, "am I close?"

"Mais ou menos … this guy I almost married, the one who didn't want to marry me when I told him I was going into medical school. Sometimes I'd see him down at Coraçao de Jesús when we went to pick up the kids. Thirty-fivish … galo/rooster … a strutter, all intensely self-involved. I get the image of all this energy that would have been directed toward changing me. Like the family. There's this blank outline called The Ideal Brazilian Woman, and I'm supposed to adapt myself to filling it. The women … maybe they'd all like to walk out and see the world, see anything beyond Blumenau, Florianópolis, Joinville, so I'm temptation for them. And for the men I'm defiance," says Bernadette, very much the general, sharp, bitter, but the general, and then all of a sudden looking sharply at Elizete, "What am I to you?"

"To me you're defiance," laughs Luiz, then seriouses up, "If you know how unstable all the structures are. I mean what needs conformity/ orthodoxy is insecurity/instability … "

Elizete, this low, easy-on-the-ears cocktail voice.

"Maybe to me you are a little temptation. I mean to have my whole life depend on my husband's English as a Foreign Language score … I mean it's his Ph.D., his exams, his trip. I'm a little shadow off in the wings someplace. And maybe I'd like to mother HERE. Or in Brasilia with my family. This whole thing about the US … "

"And the scandal of implied … you know … " smiles Luiz, "there's not a lot between women in Brazil, but men … I think if I really knew the dimensions … "

"So they've even got to that?" asks Magda.

"I tell you," says Elizete, "you're THE main topic out at the beach this summer."

"Maybe I'll get my passport this week," says Bernadette, her little face 'hard' again, this trajectory out into softening, flowering, and then back, somebody else's (non-) genetic coding for her.

"See, it's easier to end up in the house by yourself, you never have to think, just listen. There really isn't any you, just the family … "

And that night, in the rustling bamboo-outside-the-window-wind she's in this little tower-room (Hospital da Caridade operating room), no out, black walls that keep bringing them in, all the tumours, all over the faces and in the eyes, the necks, breasts, bellies, anuses, all over the skin, all over the head, and she has to keep operating and her name is Doctor and she doesn't have any hair and because she doesn't have any hair she doesn't have any shampoo or perfume, or Indian clothes, wings, the whole operating 'suit' has caked, grown on her skin.

If there is Design, if breast-feeding does have a haemostatic effect on the uterus, why these bulging eyes and deformed heads and faces?

Who's out there stalking in the night?

Family

(stalking)

"Design."

## xxxiii.

"I don't know what to do, I'm so tired all the time," says Nona, Magda's eyes drifting across the alcohol-bottles on the window-ledge filled with caranguejo spiders, giant roaches, wasps, household bugs that she's been collecting for fun (espanto/horror).

"You'll be OK once you get back to the North Pole out of this jungle," says Magda.

And that afternoon she buys her a pre-birthday gift, a leopard-spotted nightgown with the breasts in flesh-coloured lace, inverted open V just above the belly button.

It works.

She leopards for hours.

After love says, "It's funny, all the juices are uma delicia/a real treat when I'm well … nojo/disgust becomes delight."

And then it runs down. They could crucify Christ on the TV-screen and she wouldn't see it. She burrows into sleep. She's going back already, voyaging South, North, the poles are life and the equator a shore of overabundantly life-infested allergic death …

## xxxiv.

The island-ship sails into Spring, but then sails back (South wind) into Winter.

Bernadette's doing breast-reductions now, the last run toward money before she drops out altogether.

Grey *andante cantabile* afternoon.

"It's an afternoon Tchaikovsky would have liked," says Magda.

"Your taste," sneers Bernadette.

"How big were they this morning?" asks Nona.

Bernadette concaves her hands half a meter off her chest.

"Like ten kilo bags of sugar."

"I'd never get mine reduced," says Magda.

"They get monstrous," says Bernadette, "it becomes more than cosmetology, it's freakishness ... "

They're making purses, Nona and Bernadette. Nona's are coming out (dyed string) Amerindian clenched-fist strong, Bernadette's *fin de siècle* Parisian – lace, satin, satin, lace, with the addition of glinty little multi-faceted beads. Magda looking at them. Bernadette is model aeroplane scale. She pulls her hair back and she becomes the essence of a 1900 Paris whorehouse fastidious delicacy. You can just see her world centre around leg-textures, powders, tones, cat-eyes staring insouciantly at nuances of light.

And Nona is massive, even sick now with bronchitis-asthma, still massively fleshy, Renaissance heavy, when Mind still clung to Earth inside the dream of pagan fleshiness.

And herself, looking into the mirror at night, she's mannequin twenty again, youth is in flesh tension, age in looseness/sag, twenty, and the eyes stare back at her with startled ... she hesitates to call it innocence. Half a head-turn and the slavic jaw appears. Stocky dumpling grandma on the back porches of cracking-wood Chicago winters, one picture she especially remembers, grandma in her sealskin coat and what looked like a medieval Japanese horsehair cone (actually straw) hat, heavy legs and laced ("service") shoes, and Magda herself in wool coat and leggings. She had this Pekinese (in her arms in the photo) Toto. She remembered the touch of the fur on her face and arms, the little red tongue. Granddaughter merging into the image of grandmother. Like she always told Bernadette, "This body, this fat, even the hunger that produces the fat, in the thousand generations that this body was evolved in, only those who could fatten up with next to nothing survived ... "

Bernadette's purse today all black quilted-beaded satin.

"The family's becoming a real pain. They're all so curious about 'the Americans' and leaving Medicine. It's like leaving the priesthood. But they won't talk to me about it. They'll talk behind my back, but when I come around they all sit there agonizing … "

"Well, they love you," says Nona, "it's solicitude more than control … "

"But solicitude is control," says Bernadette.

"Should I tell you the truth?" asks Magda.

They're on the bed, the purse-factory's on the bed. Magda, foam-pillowed legs up, sits on this bamboo rocking chair.

"How deep does the knife go in?" asks Bernadette.

"All the way to the backbone," says Magda, "to and through, pinned wiggling on the wall. Maiden Aunt. Every family has one or two or three. They're always thin and 'careful.' Glass menagerie. They develop quirks, they're deaf or they've got eczema. They've got their chair. They collect paper-bags, their voices are always shrill, their arms and legs like bugs. You look in their eyes and, well, if they're young … no, even when they're young, there's never desire, just infinity. Their eyes infinity signs (she draws on a piece of wrapping-paper on the table next to her chair) of 'loss,' the mark of loss on their foreheads, and everyone treats them like eunuchs, third-class citizens, asexual losers, eccentrics. All their sisters and sisters-in-law, their nieces and grand-nieces are breasts, milk, vaginal drippings, even divorced, even 'abused,' they're fulfilled, but the maiden aunts, everyone imagines they're storing up treasures. They don't eat, spend, they live on air and accumulate treasures. They don't 'want,' they don't want clothes or roast-pork, they're birdseed nibblers, you can always hit 'em for a buck or for baby-sitting, but you never really open up to them either, they've got this chaste-nunnish ecclesiastical aura about them and you always distance yourself from them. They always feel what they are: hermit freaks in the world of familial touch and solidarity. They're charity cases, chronic poor souls, handouts, maybe a touch of painful 'duty,' but I suppose the worst part is 'distance,' brittle, dry-straw fragile distance, sinking into the Great Dark the way you lived, mainly untouched, unsecreted, unused, atrophied. UN, that's the centre, un-every-thing. And that's OK with everyone, you can be UN/non forever, but you start taking on colour, coming alive, the porcelain starts to flesh-out and breathe, and then everyone gets threatened … "

"That's it," says Bernadette, angry. When she talks when she's cross her nose gets hooked, her chin juts up, her voice gets strangled and shrill. "That's it. I could go out on the street and get anyone … ANY-ONE … tudo bem/all OK … it's inside the pattern, unhappy marriage is inside the pattern, separation is nao tudo bem/not OK, but acceptable. Even divorce, that's inside the pattern too. It's all centred around the Holy Roman juridical sense of legality. Nothing to do with glands. I see flies fucking and I wish I was a fly … honest to god … "

She stops.

Magda wonders, doesn't wonder, knows that all life-processes, as long as they're alive, can be reversed.

There's an equilibrium equation. She can see the fruit-bloom coming back into Bernadette's face. All she seems to do is eat, aren't dem bones starting to flesh-out, sing.

"I've got all the optimism in the world for you," says Magda, taking Bernadette's hands.

"That's how much you'll need," she answers, "I have none. Sometimes I feel that everything I say and do is just buzzing trapped inside the web."

"No, no, you're ours," says Nona and reaches over, encloses Bernadette in her Hindu-bloused arms, meat-lips against wire-hair.

As the Lear-wind blows through the bamboo-palms outside.

### XXXV.

In a Chinese restaurant over shrimps and chicken, Nona suddenly seeing Bernadette, the brilliant rat-eyes finely outlined in black, the lips dark purple, garnet-hanging (pendentes) earrings.

"The doctor's gone," she says, "really, you're a Louis Napoleon courtesan … that's what I always think they must have looked like … "

Fine, careful, deadly, spidery, cerebral, with an underlay of ushy, gushy, self-digesting, immolating "mucosalness."

And here comes Paulo, Carmen's little lost boy husband. Out on the town for dinner (Carmen in Peru, vacationing with Ari, the psychiatrist) alone.

"Oh, no," says Magda.

"Oh, yes," says Bernadette, as Paulo little lost boy ("Can I join you?") sits down.

### xxxvi.

The island sailing into summer and the Argentinians start to arrive, corpulent, belligerent, 'educated,' 'civilized' and crabby-arse. They seem more like Romans than South Americans.

Nona, she's always had these awful, hacking, body-wracking colds, but now she lies around half-dead all evening, all day, limp, and this smell, it's like shit coming out of her mouth.

"This tightness," she says, fingering into the apex of the rib cage.

Diaphragm? thinks Magda, Bernadette sits there, watching the agony, crocheting, not saying anything. Then finally …

"We ought to go and see a lung-man tomorrow. There's a Doctor Costa who's very good, a friend of mine … "

"OK," lying there in the sweaty heat, her hair plastered wet around her head, puffy, tumescent, wet-chalk skin.

"Lie on your stomach," says Magda.

"There's a yoga exercise for clearing out the lungs," says Bernadette. Nona hardly moves. "Maybe we should really start doing daily yoga … "

You can feel her in the gathering-force dark, going out, down, going weak, sliding further into loss-of-self, confusion, un-realness.

"Maybe we should call an ambulance, take her into emergency."

"Maybe," agrees Bernadette, but they watch, wait, suffer into the unreal past-midnight, into numb, disembodied pre-dawn, dawn, as she slowly betters, then a little after dawn, amid cockcrows and dog-barks, they fall asleep …

Beclosol spray, Aeroflux Edulito, a lime-coloured liquid, and this other spray, Bricanyl. She's supposed to aerosol her lungs all day.

"I'm not sure if it's asthma or bronchitis," the doctor tells her, "I'd like to see you in the middle of an attack. The general symptomology is so close."

Nona doesn't want to take anything.

"All the women in my family live to ninety-five," she keeps saying.

"You're the exception," says Magda, irritated, disgusted, "I've never heard anything 'prouder' in my life … "

"I'm afraid," says Nona, starts to cry, "I've never been so afraid before in my life. I can feel it closing down. I get afraid … "

And there she is, all blubbery and babyish, infantile latex nursery despair.

"Come on, come on," says Magda, arms around her back and shoulders, Bernadette curiously aloof, calm, an observer not (really) involved …

The next day Bernadette and Magda go downtown together, leave Nona at home. They stop off in this new snack-bar/beer-joint (on De Grau) that reminds Magda of East Lansing, and, in fact, the owner's son studied at Stanford. The first time she went in there and asked her if she were Argentinian and she told him "No, American," he started brittly teetering on in English, and now (two times later) they were old friends.

A bottle of Brahma Chopps, a table in the back. It's two in the afternoon and they aren't even open yet, but they're not just let in but welcomed.

"I really get worried about Nona," says Magda, "I mean if she clamps down, really, really clamps down, you die from a heart-attack, don't you, you strangle, asphyxiate, explode inside."

"It's like someone putting a cord around your neck and garrotting you … "

"Only why now? She's 'down,' I mean not just during an attack, but in general … "

"What do you think?"

"I think sometimes that you've been really living with us for a month, and that the time coincides. I mean she can say she wants it three-way, but I feel this undertone, I don't know, melancholy, resentment. Maybe you and I are too close … ?"

"It's something I've thought of too. I mean 'couples' are more normal, any kind of communalness is always next to impossible. We're EGO aren't we, and, after all, you and I began together 'confessing' in a way, all our secrets, I never had that with her. I mean she came into it after we'd been 'pacted,' sealed."

"And she has a real problem with feeling 'outside,' like she tries to have friends in Michigan, but if they're straight, two women living together a hundred years ago … we could have been two old maids, that's the advantage of the marginal old maid syndrome, but two women living together manless and with children … and if the friends are gay, then there's usually that 'restlessness,' and exclusivity. I'm always there. I think she really loves you, if you could just give her more … "

"OK, but with you it's easier, you're such a … "

"Shameless idiot … I know … confessional, streaming consciousness … Mississippi River-down-to-the-Gulf-of-Mexico mind."

"And she's like me, kind of all locked up and her key is in a drawer someplace and the drawer's locked up and my key's hidden on a black string hanging down between my breasts at the level (a altura de) of my heart … "

"With very special love … " Magda catching a glance at herself in a mirror on this column next to her, the eyes OK, but the neck horrible, this Neanderthal forward thrust of the neck on top of this massive thorax, envying the imp-Irish, the thin black Watusi, the tiny, boney pornographic Parisians, the bone blonde Norwegians/East Prussians … and how does a Pavlova emerge out of the Slavic nations at all … ? Genetic import?

She wants to go back on another stockings search, extra-large, black, grey, hide the blue in the legs. If there's any left. Everything is in falta/out of stock. The Argentinians are eating everything all up, buying up all the bras and big stockings, beefy beef-eaters.

"Onde estão as crianças?/Where are the kids?" a woman on the street outside. Why don't they tie strings around the fucking kids, Magda thought. She must have heard Onde estão as crianças a hundred times in the last two or three weeks …

Into the hot, bright centre of Florianópolis, the Calçado, there's this islander making a canoe out of a log, and two old ladies in a grass hut, making pots, the island of Santa Catarina for centuries just that, islands, inhabited with fishermen from the Azores, primitive, isolated, drug- and witch-centred, lost in tropical time.

And then bridges and airports were built and island as island disappeared and little by little the little, wrinkled, brown, wolf-haired proto-Mediterraneans are being replaced/transformed by the invasion of electronic, highrise New-Think that takes the millennial lifeways of the fuck-shit-eat-sleep people and turns them into "quaintly folkloric."

Five o'clock and Magda has one pair of extra-grande dark-brown stockings (Beverly – Industria de Meias Myrop) and that's all. Tudo em falta/nothing left. It really is the half-termite Argentinians. Magda loves love in stockings. For her legs are erotic organs and just skin is unmayonnaised potato-salad. Love is theatre, nuance, subtlety, a Kabuki act of symbolic heightened awareness, a meditation on Now, and all the creams, scents, stockings, anklets, hair, makeup, camisoles are the wardrobe of her Bed Mass, the consecrated sacred centre of every (circular) twenty-four hours. Bernadette and Magda walk over to Dr Carmen's office for a little silicon injection to help get rid of the wrinkles between her eyes. Marisa the receptionist smiles when she sees them. "Como vai ... tudo bem?/How's it going? Everything OK?" The office is filled. Carmen always takes on these extra patients at the end of the day, and you take one look at them and wonder what they could possibly have wrong, all these clacketty, perfect Brazilians with the perfect (sun-leathered) skin ...

They're last, of course, because they're free ... friends. It's six o'clock and Marisa leaves with a guitar in her hand, such a pretty, young wavy-haired thing with such a bright, brilliant smile. Magda made the mistake one day of asking her if she was in college or was going to go to college. No, no, no, she protested, she was in love (enamorado), not quite engaged (noivos), Magda confused, still not quite understanding the class and value structures, never quite getting it in her head that vertical mobility was next to zero. Then Carmen came out all East Indian skirted and smiling, brought them into her office.

"Que sopresa!/What a surprise!"

But not really. She had been Bernadette's former office-mate before Bernadette decided to strike it out on her own.

Bernadette very much at home, helps with the syringe, the injection, Magda much more comfortable and secure in Bernadette's than in Carmen's hands, the frown disappearing, Magda for a moment believing in the eternality of the body, daily resurrection.

"We're meeting Nona and the kids at six-thirty at Sol da Terra," says Magda, looking (happily) in the office mirror, "You want to come along?"

"Great … "

And they go out into the purple-sprinkling dusk to find Nona there (second floor balcony) with the kids, waiting.

Soup of the Day, Pizza, Juices, Crumbly Healthcake …

"It's true about the Africans on grain and whole-grain diets … these enormous loads of you know what … and no varicose-veins or stomach cancer," says Magda.

"Oh, I'm a devotee," says Carmen, "You don't have to convince me … " then to Nona, "How are you?"

"This awful, unexplained sudden worsening of asthma … "

"Unexplained, but not necessarily unexplainable," says Carmen, "I mean stress, if you go into the psychological roots of things, analyse the total psychosomatic picture. It's like with dermatology, psychological states can cause all kinds of skin problems."

"Yeah, we were talking about that this afternoon," says Magda.

"What?" asks Nona, wet-chalky, working at breathing, like shovelling, drawing water out of a well, angry.

"What's wrong?" asks Magda.

What's wrong indeed? Remembering back to Paul and Carole Ferlazzo, Nona throwing them out of the house one time, accusing the three of them of conspiring against her.

"What were you saying about me this afternoon?"

"Just that this whole three-way-ness of things might not really, really, really suit you, and … "

"I'm not crazy, if that's what you mean. And I'm not imagining things."

"But the mind/imagination can be a psychosomatic 'trigger,'" says Bernadette, getting all nervousy too. Magda hating it, wanting to zero in on the pizza, the juice, the vitamin biz, and ignore all this short-circuiting, the endless supersonic whine … And then later, in Magda's bedroom, Nona getting all weird again, Magda impatiently asking "What is wrong?"

"I'm not crazy, not 'imagining,'" says Nona.

"No one says you are, but there is a psychosomatic factor," says Bernadette, and Nona's suddenly up, gone, into the master bedroom, bangs the door and the next thing you can hear her bawling.

"My god," says Magda, "she hasn't done that for years," thinking about the Ferlazzos again, Nona's long-term undercurrent of paranoia, feeling that everyone is ganging up on her …

She was some sort of eternal little girl, not lost in the house on the prairies, but ignored. You had to keep it apple pie à la mode, unfurled, uncomplicated, all ploughed straight, OR ELSE …

"Why don't you go in and talk to her?" suggests Magda.

"Me no," answers Bernadette, hard, poker-faced.

So they wait … and wait … and wait … then Alexandra comes in.

"Não quero mais briga nenhuma nessa cas, viu/I don't want any more fights in this house, OK?"

And then Sarah Bernhardt Margaret.

"Mas o que está passando, é terrível … terrível/What's going on anyhow, it's terrible … terrible … "

And she starts to bawl. Magda amazed at their Portuguese. At school, and after school playing with kids on the street all afternoon, but still …

"Margaret," says Magda, containing, con-tain-ing herself with a Samurai effort, "every little fight's like moving from outer toward inner molecular rings, toward the nucleus where it's E equals m c squared … "

"O que?/What?" asks Bernadette, totally confused, a little amused.

"In other words, every fight's a little jump toward greater intimacy and bonding. Fights have their positive side."

The kids leave, five minutes later Nona comes in all embarrassed.

"I'm sorry, I don't know what's wrong with me."

"Well, the medicine might be contributing," says Magda, "you're taking a goddam barrelful of stuff every day."

"I don't know, when people start saying I'm imagining things … "

"No one says you're imagining things," says Bernadette, "but there's an emotional factor in asthma."

"And your emotional factor in this asthma," says Magda, "is fear. I mean she tightens up like a violin string. She's terrified. Which I can understand. We used to have this iron foundry next to us in Spain. Just a local little thing, imagine, right next to this apartment building. It only 'melted' (founded?) on Fridays, then this awful gas would come out of it. I got a good whiff one Friday afternoon and that night I clamped down, woke up, no breath at all, closed down, tremendous effort, it opened up … but, Jesus, I kept a respirator next to my bed for a whole year, I was so scared. It's a terrible thing."

"I'm not used to it. I've never been ill before like this. I am afraid."

"And you feel like we're conspiring, right?" smiles Magda. Nona has to smile too, embarrassed, but enjoying the intimacy of embarrassment.

"Well, aren't you … ?"

"We're worried about you," says Bernadette.

"In a sense your entire family in Kansas City is a conspiracy. Under the democratic surface there were all kinds of secret-deals, like mothers who'd been married before and not a word about it, or miscarriaged other children, sisters getting married in super-virginal white gowns fighting morning sickness at the altar, brothers legitimizing English nurse mistresses in quiet secret marriages … but always with this meat and potatoes, stars and stripes Rose Bowl forever surface … " added Magda.

"Not that my family was any different," starts in Bernadette, "my father never directly dealt with us, it was always through my mother, and then she'd 'filter' things out, so there was always this implied secrecy … "

"Well, my father's direct," says Nona, "when he talks. But he saves up talking for these pronouncements. Like the last time I was there, he made this declaration: 'WHEN I DIE, THE WORD DIES WITH ME.' Which … "

"Solipsism," says Magda to herself, suddenly outside, it's THEM talking to THEMSELVES, the whole polarisation of the room changed, they've gone into an inner ring of high intimacy, and she's still outside …

Which is OK in a way. That's what she wants is their intimacy.

It has to be shared on the most intimate levels. She and Bernadette can't just pair up, it has to be all a trio from now on. And she and Bernadette have been getting a bit too paired-up and not including Nona inside.

She gets up, is hardly noticed when she says she's going to take a bath. She's burning, as close as she can get to boiling herself alive.

Into the bathroom, in love with death as the water steams into the tub, the water all wildly bubbling with Village Strawberry bathsalts, Nona's birthday gift from her Aunt Mabel. That's really what her wanting to get a facelift is all about too, isn't it – some sort of flirtation with Death, wanting Death to get her definitively on her Back, not wait for Him to come, but actively seek out his deliciousness, go down with 'class' and Samurai bravery … Toe in the water. Burning. Leg burning. Whole body burning. A total immersion in burning, and when her skin got used to it and took the burning as normal, then adding some more hot water, one more level in toward the (resurrection) I am Energy nucleus …

### xxxvii.

"I've always wanted a business," Nona is saying. Lunch. Sonia's made the usual – a brown rice main dish with chicken and peas and tomatoes and shredded cheese, then hot tuna fish with onion, heavily mayonnaised potato-salad, maracujá juice made with almond-blossom honey, whole wheat bread, coffee, "I mean not always, always, there was a time when I wanted to be inside. But I got the Ph.D. and polished up the handles on the big front door … "

"Polished what?" interrupts Bernadette.

"It's a Gilbert and Sullivan reference," Magda starts to explain.

"Gilbert and Sullivan?"

"It means that if you do the menial jobs, you do well in the way of the world," says Nona, sipping her second glass of maracujá, Sonia sitting there staring at them, not understanding a word, "I got the Ph.D., even got an article published based on my dissertation. It was all open sea, and then the 1970 slump hit ... and then no more permanent what they call tenure-track jobs ... "

"Concursos para profesores titulares," 'Brazilianized' Magda.

"So I'd get three classes sometimes, sometimes two ... sometimes they'd tell me a week ahead of time, sometimes a couple of days. They'd hire a black guy from Harvard because there was a black-hiring quota so federal funds wouldn't get cut off ... "

"O governo federal castiga universidades e outras organizações com a retirada de fondos federais se não contratem uma certa porcentagem de pretos/ the federal government punishes universities and other organisations with the withdrawal of federal funds if they don't contract a certain percentage of blacks ... " explains Magda.

Sonia's ears prick up. She likes the idea.

"And no future, no promises ... hopes ... just more of the same, the department's full of these permanent temporaries ... temporary for twenty-five years ... "

"How can they be permanently temporary?" asks Bernadette.

"Because that's how they pay them less. I mean grad assistants, post-docs, temporaries, it's a bargain workforce to which the ordinary rules don't apply. Who knows, with a minimum of encouragement, pardon the corn, but fair-play, I ... "

"Pardon the corn?" asks Bernadette.

"Disculpe o sentimentalismo/Forgive the sentimentalism," translates Magda.

"Really, with a minimum of fair-play I might have ended up a scholar, heaven forbid ... but now ... "

"E eu podería ter ficado na Medicina se não fosse o INPS como é ... and I might have stayed in Medicine if the INPS wasn't the way it is ... " says Bernadette.

"The INPS ... ?" asks Nona.

"Instituto Nacional de Providencia Social," explains Bernadette, "Brazil's version of socialised medicine."

"And what's wrong with it?" Nona, the socialist, very interested.

"Like they pay by units," says Bernadette, "Like you can get twice as much money if you take one tonsil out one day and another tonsil out the next day. So that's what people start to do. One varicose leg stripped one day, the another the next day. And if you have to give an extra pint of blood you've got to justify that because it's not in the computerised 'need-programme' for a particular operation. And a surgery that takes six hours gets the same amount as sixty minutes, and Caesarians get paid more than natural birth, so they become matter-of-course ... and there's no professional nurses except the chief nurse, so you get a bunch of operating room flunkies getting paid a thousand dollars a year, so they can't have any higher education, can they, if the infrastructure is 'corrupt' that can't be unrelated to the superstructure. You can't start building at the tenth floor. It's an unjust, unreal bureaucratic maze created by disembodied theoreticians … "

"Of course, isn't most of the world," says Magda, who's eating just yoghurt and peanuts, very involved in this everyday-more-intense dash/plunge/scream into 'Health' by Bernadette, "I think the woman in both of you wants out and it can't come out in these male institutions that see people as work-units. Where's the nurseries in the office-buildings and factories? Where's the womb-/mother-part in the eight hour day? You're supposed to leave mother at home, aren't you, and menstrual you is all covered up so they cover up the children too. Dirty words. The perfect woman worker's some kind of sterile, titless, wombless hands and brain, nothing in between. Although the whole work-structure could be redesigned around whole people instead of just utilitarian workers … "

"Even in Spain," adds Magda, "even in Spain they've started this kindergarten mania where they stick the kids in 'school' from two or three years on. Another generation and all that sense of deep family bond … it just won't be the same. It'll get Henry Fordish, the Great Ford'll rule all," Magda letting the 60s kaleidoscope through her, Be-Ins, Love-Ins, the King of Echo-Park, naked to a flowered waist, a crown of flowers on his head, handing a much younger her a red rose, a long-haired topless blonde surrounded by black bongo-drummers, dancing, the peacock-people, the rose and hollyhock people, headbanded and beaded and high … souls moving through this clairvoyant green crystal-ball world, "Do you really think business will be any better than Medicine or the university?"

"I think so," says Nona, and the Wait (inside Magda) begins, customers, the interpersonal expectations, you sensitively make your purses, cut your jewels, they're your perfect children, and then the nurseryed factory-world children come in with their suspicious faces and unlinked-to-you eyes, the mystique of their world filters into yours and your precious things become theirs, they wanna good deal, it all becomes hard money and their bionic fingering, judging, rejecting/even accepting all galls … Magda remembering one time up in João Pessoa, this little Artesanata Pavilion, this hard-rock blonde from São Paulo, all these idiot questions, "Is this from here? I don't think it's from here. I think it's from Amazonas. Will it last? What kind of wood? Is it handmade or machine?" It was getting Magda all acidy, and when she left, Magda asked the woman in the stall "How do you stand it?" "Perguntas da clientela/customer-questions," said the owner unperturbed … but not really …

71

"Don't worry," says Magda to the sad faces around the table, "It'll all be maternal. Milk and wombs. World as love and reproduction … "

"Well, that's really all that makes any sense," says Nona, and Bernadette concurs.

### xxxviii.

"How do you begin to become gay?" I mean have you always been?" asks Magda, dawn just beginning to filter in through the shutters.

"I really don't think I am," says Bernadette, "I just like YOU, and you just happen to be female … "

### xxxix.

"I don't know," says Magda over evening coffee, "I went into your bedroom last night and looked at you and the girls – I always check for spiders and that you're breathing OK – and I stood watching the girls, especially Margaret, and I couldn't get over how big she is, what a woman … and I started to cry. And then this morning Alexandra comes in with her drawer full of treasures, a 'heel' of flawed tourmaline, a Fofoleta dolla, a handkerchief, some drawings, an old key … I don't know, what's the pattern, I'm feeling TIME pass, and I'm seeing myself re-growing up, and it's so far back I've forgotten that an earlier me ever existed. Or do I feel their growing-up crowding me, their moving toward maturity meaning that I'm moving toward … "

A swallow of coffee, a fragment of bread buttered and honeyed and ingested. Like a lizard with a fly.

### xl.

This is all I want, thinks Magda, her mouth full of the copper taste of Bernadette, Bernadette's mouth on her copper-mouth, the feel of her nylon camisole against her rump and the curve of her nyloned legs. You've got to UP sensitivity, mucosa on mucosa becomes so nuanced/shaded, smoke on charcoal, cacao on canela, sand. Close down the Outside at midnight and pull night's cape in around you, bloodlight and flick a touch of fingercymbal sandalwood-patchouli fragrancing behind each ear.

TV is evil, FM, BBC World News.

"I'll tell you why I like New Orleans whorehouses circa 1900, you walk through the doors and that's the point, you leave the world outside. I mean your dead husband or your crippled daughter or business failure or your stutter, you hate the pea-soup green of your living room walls, you were 'abused' as a child, whatever … the big events become powder and shades, nipples and textured legs, the gleam of a black satin corset or green eyeshadow above a startled eye … "

Midnight and you contract in on yourself.

"Narcissism is the ultimate sanity. Altruism is crusades and crusades are slaughters in which ideas slit the throats of infants … "

Midnight and you walk into the unashamed brown-black mirror, assume poses of rump and leg-line, breasts fall into black lace sags, you pout and kiss your own glass-flesh, and then you're inside with arms/mouth around the (copper) Other.

"You find the Other inside your deepest, darkest you … "

Your nipples are black down wings that float you up into the gostoso/delicious night sky.

How can pumping legs become so spongily "aware," and the awareness spreads up through the anus and enters into the Grotto of Consummation and webs and nets stretch through the walls, as you focus down on the white acetylene point at the centre of the black-petalled night, the black onyx tooth at the centre of white beating daydreams.

"Monastic isolation was/is the basis for any kind of 'sanity.' I remember Easter up in, where was it, Sheboygan, Wisconsin, this Benedictine monastery, no-talk, cold stone Easter, and then the fleshy lily-look and smell , the 'melting' of the Resurrection. But without the withdrawal you never get the flowering, it just all stays muddled and flat … "

The feel of hair around your face. She touches it. You feel it. Pressure, fluff-halo, and the ribs begin to emerge (yoghurt-peanuts), the raison d'etre of everything becomes the Centre of Night.

It's all body, the hang of breasts becomes divine, the pull-in of the diaphragm, the sinew-lines of straining legs. You look up from love into the wall mirror and your black-purple lipstick's all gone, but your eyes stare out of your blonde face like a lynx after a kill, surprised and startled by a camera.

"All the metaphors of Love-Death, Sanctity-Ecstasy/Orgasm run true. Which is why I sometimes believe in immortality, which seems to be only an extension of the finding of self in self-loss, filling in evacuation."

You lie back, you should be exhausted but you aren't. You're looking down at yourself from the ceiling, the mask-eyes staring up, everything erect and waiting, and you don't want it to stop.

Then a rooster crows through the early morning rain. Enemy day, the day-things waking that don't prey on Others under the cover of vampire-night, but only vegetate abstractly planning day-revenge and the turning of Earth into a Holocaust of Honour …

## xli.

They've got the TV on (Chacrinha) but sound off. If anything good/interesting comes on, they turn it up. Chacrinha the Ridiculous, he looks eighty, all dressed like a baby tonight, all these beautiful dancers in lycra leotards and tops that show underarm, under-breast and crotch sweat-areas, and instead of high heels/high-heeled boots (it's Tuesday – Chacrinha's Amateur Hour) that they wear on the Saturday night discoteca show, they're all wearing tennis shoes. There's a singer front stage centre and two skate-boarders are sliding out around him as one of the Chacrettes (Magda – long, thick hair, intelligent face, a body as juicy as a ripe cashew-fruit) comes out and starts to weave around him, the whole effect rendered absurd by the fact of the tennis shoes.

"Mainly Lúcio was a liar," the other Magda's saying, "it was easier for him to lie than not. I mean I wasn't even concerned about other women, although I think that 'proving himself' periodically was/is an important part of his identity reinforcement.

"Only what happens if he fails ... ? He gets some young thing in bed and it doesn't happen, what does he do, 'eliminate' the witness to his shame? I mean it's a terrible thing, the Unicorn Olympics. I mean a bowl of jelly doesn't have to prove anything. It's like those Hindu vulva-statues, woman as receptor. The onus is on the stag. And if the stag doesn't perform it's a Greek tragedy. One thing I never worried about one way or the other was 'getting it.' He was always going out and buying houses and things without telling me. Separate bank accounts, separate 'friends.' We lived next to his university in California and I had to commute forty-five miles each way to mine. How can I put it ... he was so programmed, I mean culturally programmed. Not that I wasn't, but with a difference ... I could step out of myself and identify what was ME and what was imposed on ME. He couldn't. He thought he was his culture. Whatever stupid macho idiot things Peru imposes on its males, that's him. If it's in the code to pinch arses, then that's you, arse-pinching is the essential you. Who can live with that?"

"But why specifically did you break up?" asks Bernadette.

"Immune reaction, anti-body formation. I, like, would want to talk about something, grieve as in grievance/grievance-committee, readjust accounts, interact, exchange ideas. And he just wouldn't. 'Let's talk about Cecilia, I found this letter in one of her notebooks. She's thirteen and sleeping around', I'd say, and get back something like 'She'll get married in a white gown, that's all that counts.' That kind of flip response. I got to the point where I didn't even want to touch him, and then along comes Nona, and ... "

"Had you ever had women lovers before?"

"Well … implied, potential, the only thing we didn't do we DO … and in fact with her I never really planned anything, and then afterwards I wondered why it had taken me so long … "

"I'm still kind of avergonhada … ashamed … " says Nona.

"Thanks!"

"Well, you want me to be honest. Out There's still Out There. I wish it wasn't, but … my parents and sisters, I suppose they really can't put a name on it like that, but … for them … well, people live together, don't they, what happens behind walls … aren't you?" Nona asks Bernadette.

"Aren't I what?"

"Ashamed."

She gives one of her screwed-up-nose disdainful wicked-witch-of-the-West looks.

"De que?/Of what?"

"Of being an outsider?"

"Outside what?"

"But you – never were, I mean, 'gay' before, were you?"

"No, just 'hurt,' I was normal and hurting, now I'm abnormal and not hurting."

Magda sitting there wondering and wondering, how can she and Nona have been together for so many years and still managed to achieve so little 'adjustment.' Scratch that, substitute 'acceptance.' How about just entregando-se, surrendering to the currents of inevitability, the floodtides of necessity. The waters come, the stars fall, the fire descends, the oceans rise out of their beds and the earth's crust begins to crack, you sit down, you bow you head and se entrega, surrender yourself, unwitnessed, with a dignity whose meaning doesn't extend beyond its own private grace.

"No, I look back," says Bernadette, "I had this one abortion, which was the centre of madness. The first surrender, the second, the whole series, expecting to find soil to grow in, and I never did, until now. The whole world out there so 'alien,' no money for food and housing, always money for wars, nuclear amoebas hungry to devour each other, the mysteries of inflation and the predestined necessity of cars, rules and laws and theory-systems that have nothing to do with real streets and real bedrooms … "

The weather nods back and forth, day to day, hour to hour. This afternoon it's a cold blustering wind, tonight what will it blow in, the vaginal ooze of Bahia black Spring?

## xlii.

You begin on the level of John Derrick, shuffle papers, suck on a pipe, rattle around on computer keys, read D.H. Lawrence and imagine you're the Counsel in *Under the Volcano*, Byronically misunderstood, supersensitively "aware" in a tropical Eden populated by arseholes. All pride inside the maze of blind bureaucracy.

Then suddenly you're just people among people, in the mansion on the top of a hill on a poverty-stricken street where the kids next door have fleas (the lovemaking begins, the lingam-incense snaking out into the red cobra night, touch and more touch, the pulling out into Here) and the name-calling Guerra dos Piolhentos/War of the Flea-Infested begins. Katia, the girl next door rings the bell to see Alexandra.

"Did you call me a Piolhenta?"

"Well, you are!"

And Katia slaps Alex across the mouth. It's all shacks huddled up the rump of the hill, kids with ballpoint pen thin legs. Ten and they look like five, five and they look like three. And illiterate Donna Betty who uses the radio and sun to tell time (Hands/lips descending to nipples and between legs, sweetly pulling you – imperiously – into the irritation of the incense, and rooms and "real" faces vanish, you open your eyes and begin to be, legs and black mask eyes staring out jaguar-startled into the impossibility of this room and this reality.) All the expense and bother of screens and then Sonia leaves the unscreened windows open and there's not a night you don't have to suffer before you uneasily sleep your malarial encephalitic sleep.

All the talk about choking (allergies) and Nona's nightly night-crises. And then Sonia will wax the floors because wax is salvation, the jewelled City of God has waxed floors. Mum and your robot childhood disappear.

"All I want is this," you cry to yourself when you're finally alone in your own bed in your own room. Really cry because you feel you've been robbed, forty-eight years and have you had even eight hours really alive before now?

Waves of black light, mercury-light on aggressive purple. You boil, steam, vaporise, vapour-like white, churning bowels, you're Lady be Good sound and colour-swirls, x-rayed, charred, pulverized and then blown (coating) all over the walls of your essence of night room.

"I wish I had sperm," says Magda after it's over, "it'd be our flesh and blood. Just think of that miracle, our flesh. I'd never have an abortion. In fact I always knew when I was ovulating, they were children before I even fucked. I lived in the total awareness of myself as creator ... "

Hands soothing, coming "down," airfoil wings coasting down to the beaches of their respective skins.

"Lúcio always hated Cecilia, from the first baby pictures on. She looked almost 'black,' crispy hair … and blacks in Peru are all 'sambos,' there's all these ruthless jokes about 'sambos' and 'cholos,' Indians and Chinos, jokes about everyone but the upper middle and upper class. Which, of course, is mainly white. Maybe there was a mulata grandmother somewhere in his family. Buried somewhere deep under the roots of the family tree. And me, I love a nice racial mix, hate white-white skin. And then Marcella was born and she had this butter-bright hair, unreal, like a wig. Some Hungarian blood in Lúcio's family way, way back. And we'd be travelling through Mexico, Tehuantepec, and the Indians on the bus, I mean middle class Indians, you know, acculturated, we'd get to a town and they'd say 'Can we take the little one home with us for a while?' OK. No problem, and she'd come back with an ice-cream in her hand and her hair all full of ribbons. And Cecilia zero, no attention except negative attention. Bow-legged, like Marilyn Monroe. I always liked the way she was, but Lúcio ganged up on her, him and the other kids. It was like a fucking conspiracy. And Lúcio junior, the boy, my son … was blondish too … Peru's like a 1940s movie, nothing really 'alien' about it when it comes to middle-class shit-headed values. The good old days, my arse! I'll tell you what the good old days were – Bourgeoise Fascism, be Middle Class or else! That's Lúcio's essence, traditional values, cows and bulls, black and white, the Code of the Computerised Cowboy … "

Bernadette sleeping, smiles in her sleep. Orgasm's ON, confession's OFF.

Magda wished she felt tired.

Night, bat-mosquitos, her wide-away eyes and nerves keep saying to fly away …

She will, of course, won't she, again and again and again, fly away … alone … again …


### xliii.

Madga alone in the big house, on the bed writing poetry, fan on. She really can't tell if it's raining outside, beyond the shutters. Over in the jungle to the left of the house someone's chopping bamboo. To the right, right next door, the old lady who lives in a shoe's feeding and singing to her dogs. Up on the top of the hill beyond the guava-stand, someone's hammering. And then there's someone (the old lady?) cutting grass.

How do you define malaise?

It's like Marion Smith's brain tumour, always saying simply "I feel weird," all the doctors in the world brushing 'weird' aside, until it finally became a diagnosable tumour.

The light in the room's the colour of lard. Things no one else thinks about.

Bare breasts, stockings, she gets up on all fours in front of the mirror and does some yoga breathe-in exercises. You spend a life hoarding threads and leathers and polishing your skin, and then (straightening up) you've got sagging breasts and a big belly and a dissolving face.

Afraid someone'll ring the bell.

The injustice of Bernadette leaving Medicine, Nona leaving the university, and sagging, Slavic wreck *her* still harnessed into the plough.

The night before she'd told Bernadette, "I see myself in a house in London. It could be Kew Gardens. Or that slightly ominous area around Sadler's Wells, light between grey and candle. Sixty, which is only twelve years away, and how many surgeries between I don't know. Blonde. Afro-curl. I've had a bellyectomy, a breast-lift, silicon injected into the wrinkles, eyes lifted here and there. I've fought and won, if you don't look too closely at the scars. I'm The Lover. You and Nona have this chain of Brazil shops, I cook, exercise, wait for you to come home. I haven't been out of the house for five years … "

Withdrawal. Who can bear the departmental round-table and John Derrick?

"You do your job and anything outside the professional, whatever else men may say, ignore it," Bernadette said.

How? They'd all gone downtown for bathing suits and ought to be home any minute now … all these people come to the big house, the mailman, the telephone-bill man, students. If anyone comes all the doors are locked and there's these big mahogany wardrobes, and the minute she thinks herself TRAPPED she understands Polanski's, what was the name of the film, Catherine Deneuve moving into homicidal catatonia …

### xliv.

"Yeah, my grandmother was a big influence on me," Nona is saying. The dayship sailing into summer now, Bernadette already anticipating "Que calor!" Nona always answering her "You think this is hot, wait until you get to Kansas City!"

"I used to sleep with her. The first twelve, thirteen years of my life I slept with her. My father was on the call board down at the railroad and sometimes he worked, sometimes he didn't, and he never knew when, so my mother had to go out and work and my grandmother was IT at home … the Centre, with all her manias about not hanging different-coloured towels up on the line together, or mixing towels and sheets, the sheets were here, the pillow-cases there, the towels a little further down on the

78

line. And she was always crocheting, knitting, sewing, cooking, cleaning, this hump on her back from a fall off a horse in Texas fifty years before, so she was always slow, careful, methodical. 'We used to get an orange once a year at Christmas.' Her mother was German. It was Prussian order transferred to the American prairies. When they first went down to Texas ... well, my grandfather was a railway builder. He built the railroads into Texas. When you think back just a hundred years, it is all Western movies, isn't it?"

"Think a hundred years into the future," smiles Magda, "it's gonna be right back where it was ... "

"In a sense when I was fifteen I had an eighty-five year old handicraft pioneer mind."

"And now?"

They're sitting in Bernadette's room, on the bed, crocheting purses, getting more and more expert, sophisticated, elaborate, the cloth becoming gold and everything getting hung with beads, the purses become wind-chimes, chandeliers, mobiles taking off into the opera-theatre festa gold-glass night on their own.

"You've always been her," says Magda, "just like I've always been my grandmother. When I walk across the kitchen floor, for god's sake ... and my whole insect-sensitivity with people. My uncle, her son, lived a block away, and she could see the bedroom window from our back porch, and they'd sleep late on Sundays. And I mean LATE. Like two in the afternoon. And you'd get my grandmother's report every fifteen minutes, like it was damnation, the Sodom-Gomorrah fires were about to descend on Chicago because of her son and his shanty-Irish sexy hopeless-housewife wife. And she'd pump my cousins for information. She could have done ... what do they call ... Time-Movement reports on my aunt's activities. And when she'd baby-sit over there, if she found mouldy clothes in the wardrobe, you know, wet to be ironed and then Gertrude would forget and leave them there ... although later, when she'd lived with Gertrude for fourteen years, after my parents more or less threw her out after my father's heart attack – good excuse – she told me 'All those years I was 'after' Gertrude, and since I moved in with them, she couldn't have been better with me, better than my own daughter.' Tears in her eyes. She cried a lot. She saw it whole, and people ... she never missed a trick. She was my professor of characterisation, Professor of Being in the World ... "

She stops and she's there for a minute, there on their island, looking out the window. The neighbours' wild chickens come clucking, foraging by.

"Maggie, come on," Nona smiles at Magda, "chicken dumplings for dinner. With all these big snakes around, who's to guess it was us ... " then turns to Bernadette and gets juridical again, "And your grandmother?"

"The purpose of grandmothers is to fill in the blanks left by absentee mothers … and/or to offset with disinterested affection the ego-trips of mothers who see themselves as commanders of behaviourist Gestapo training camps … " and then sadder, that dark flower that rises so easily to the surface of her consciousness, "I remember an old tubercular Italian mummy so pain-involved with herself that there was no way she could reach out and touch or empathise with anyone else. Of course Brazil's a grandmother, the streets are grandmothers, especially when you're a child and you're everyone's granddaughter … "

And she cries. Cries easily, although you wouldn't expect her to, she's learned role-playing so well, the doctor, the magic word 'surgeon.'

But that was before, wasn't it, before she'd shed the white coat and emerged into realtime with her pink skin bright and sensitive, like after chemical abrasion.


## xlv.

It was Nona's birthday (December 8), but … Well, there was this liquidação at Fiancée which had the nicest lingerie that Magda kept saying she had seen anywhere, and with 50% off the prices were almost bearable, and that's where Magda had got Nona's birthday present, this camisole-robe combination with the transparent lace-breasts (both robe and nightgown, two layers of veils) and she'd got one for herself too ("at these prices … " as if she were saving instead of spending), and Bernadette had squealed "E eu, eu/Me, me!" and years before in Valencia, Spain, Magda had got an elephant tusk ("endangered species, like us … ") and silver 'wedding' ring, and she remembered that over at Summertime they had some like it in the jewellery case. Not exactly the same, but …

"Let's get her a wedding ring," Magda suggested to Nona that night while Bernadette was in getting ready for the night's activities.

"OK."

So the next day they went and bought one that was almost a duplicate of the one that Magda had bought in Spain, and then in the evening … They're watching the original *Mutiny on the Bounty* and it's a hot night, especially in Magda's room.

All three of them in black nylon-lace camisoles.

Magda gets up, lights this big sandalwood candle on the dining room table, a stick of sandalwood incense, comes back in. Bernadette's ogling the Polynesians, "But were they really so beautiful?" Magda's brain cross-referencing through Gauguin's ("Soyez Heureux" – "Be Happy") faces and bodies, like Mayan god-friezes come alive.

"Even more so."

And then Bernadette's little Fox-nose pricks up with the incense.

"Que é isso? /What's that?"

"Wait for the commercials. Anyhow, all that happens now is that they escape to Pitcairn Island … where their descendants still are today," says Magda, thinking that the island of Santa Catarina isn't that different from Polynesia, the Mind (inside Brazil) different, but not the place.

Although the place is the mind it's inside …

"Mas o que é … /But what is … ?" and she gets up, goes into the dining room.

"Where's the ring?" Magda asks Nona.

"I'll get it … " and they're gathered around the candle, the kids come in (watching *Mutiny* on their own TV).

"What's happening?"

"Put out your hand," says Magda and Bernadette puts out her hand, Nona hands Magda the ring and together they stick it on Bernadette's hand.

"With this ring we do thee wed, to have and to hold, from this day forward, in sickness and health, for richer or poorer, til death us do part … OK?"

"OK," says Bernadette, red, embarrassed.

"Mas não se pode casar-se duas mulheres," says Alexandra, the little Bullhead Realist, "two women can't get married … "

"We can do anything as long as it's LOVE," says Magda, "OK?"

That makes sense to Alex.

"OK."

She's convinced.

All five embrace, the ring takes on flesh, they hold on, warmth, touch, sandalwood candle and incense sense, and also (male steel stalking through the uterine mucosal night) fear …

Back into the bedroom.

They're burning the ship on Pitcairn.

"I'd like to go there sometime," says Nona.

"We're already there," answers Magda.


### xlvi.

Bernadette's as bad as Magda in the business of money. She's accumulated a lot, and now that she's one foot and three more toes on the other foot OUT, she's got to work not to blow it all.

Fiancée again.

"There's never really enough … now that … " she says to Magda, who has just found this fuzzy black body-suit, "for the long Michigan hibernation-winters," then finding this breast-hugging, hanging-from-the-breasts gown that opens between the legs with a big vaginal V, "I have to get this," and another baby-doll for Bernadette, a nipple-out bra.

Bernadette writes the cheque.

It's been happening slowly, the funds becoming one. Magda already anticipating that they'll have to get a three-way account up there. And in a sense it's more intimate than bed, their money-sharing, and walking out into the bright sequinned afternoon with their passport to night packages, they know it.


### xlvii.

"First my father," says Nona, "the human toadstool. You can't even say he plopped himself full-time down in front of TV sports and filtered out the rest of the world, because he'd sleep through half the world series and all the bowl-games, that's the dominant image, him like a big turtle propped up asleep and snoring in front of the TV. So later when Donald came along and talked, I mean he always talked, talked, talked and talked, I guess I hardly even listened to what he was saying. From mute wall to whispering tree, that's a major change."

"But what was he saying?" asks Bernadette.

Glory-weather, just before it sweats into "tropical" it's all high and giant bowel-clouds, bamboo samuraiing in rowdy wind, oily hand-smacking banana leaves, guaba and papaya, persimmon, all start to become themselves, papaya (Mamão) all year, but the yellow-squishy Guave (Goiaba) would begin to fall in February, and in March (Fall again) the Persimmons (Cacquí) would turn to dull orange jellyfish jelly. The year in adolescence now, defining itself, and the call to definition came through the afternoon windows, Bernadette making a khaki art-deco leaf-patterned velvet purse and Nona a black and gold. They'd found a place in downtown Florianópolis that had said "There's no limit as to how many we'll buy. We're going to re-sell them in Rio."

"He was mainly saying that he had all the answers. John God ... you know ... "

"John ... ?"

"It's so hard to describe. He'd get a prize for surface. He never hit me, was never 'unfaithful,' although lots of times I wished he would have been, he never was late for work ... "

"He sounds good."

Nona getting all screwed-up, tense.

"That bamboo's so noisy," she says, "sometimes at night it sounds like an army advancing toward the house."

"But what about Donald?" Bernadette insists.

"He's the kind of guy who would go through a supermarket figuring per-unit pieces on canned goods and then buying exclusively on the basis of the per-unit price."

"Como é?/What exactly?"

"Like one jar of peanut butter would be a dollar for ten ounces, another a dollar fifteen for fourteen ounces. He'd carry a calculator around with him and figure how much per ounce, and automatically buy the cheapest ... "

"But that's logical ... "

"Only there's differences in quality ... it's not just all money ... "

Magda comes in. She's been sitting in her room trying to read *Grande Sertão: Veredas*, but the voices fly in like blue butterflies.

"Well, one night I invited them over for dinner, and afterwards I guess it was Donald who started talking about religion, Does God Exist, something like that ... and Donald went on and on, Nona tried to talk – at the time she was a dyed-in-the-wool practicing Congregationalist – Donald would interrupt her ... like

Nona:     The world has design ...
Donald:  As I was saying, God represents the supreme creation of the human imagination. When you think of the thousands and thousands of books about this something that doesn't exist, it's frightening. It shows how a Hitler can happen. The mind creates A REALITY, the reality then takes on a life of its own ...
Nona:     But the World as Design is real, doesn't that inevitably lead to a Designer CAUSE ... ?

and Donald wouldn't even answer her. He'd go on about the voyage of the Beagle or 'Even Teilhard de Chardin finally had to admit that there's a self-developing, self-complicating mechanism in Nature itself.' What made him so odious was that the punishment was always on this microscopic scale. I mean The Smile covered all sins ... "

"Like," says Nona, "he'd do exactly what Magda's just done ... explain me to someone else instead of letting me explain myself ... "

"Well, deary," says Magda, "you weren't doing a very good job on your own ... "

"See what I mean? The only difference is that you're a clown."

Looking in the wall mirror ... all these months of semi-fanatic vegetarianism, the face slimming and self-defining. If it wasn't for the trace of beginning jowls ...

"Not so much so any more."

"Really," says Bernadette, hands around Magda's waist, prodding into her belly.

"Once the jowls are pulled tight again, a star can be re-born – at fifty ... "

Clowning, turning, slithering back, all black balletic with black suede boots, summer coming meaning the (hateful) shedding of her black nylon skin ... Three hours later, the kids are watching *Picapau Amarelo* on TV and they're getting hungry. Nona's got a corn-bread cooling on the dining-room table. The coffee's already made and thermosed, all that has to be done is to warm the milk. The khaki velvet purse is finished except for the addition of the beads that Bernadette does with surgical slowness like she's sewing up the eye of a salamander, Nona's still doing the hem of her black lace purse. The final touches/acabamento.

"No, I lack physical activity," Bernadette's saying, "ballet ... yoga ... it's my religion I suppose, the cult of keeping in total shape. And it's a big need. A need to move. And maybe the need for a little alone-time ... privacy ... "

"My problem," Nona answers, "is that I can't 'relate.' I mean I'm butter to be churned, never the churner. Guava asserts itself, and, my god, the assertiveness of the bamboo, but me, no ... sometimes I think I'm the Little Girl Who Never Became ... "

"Became what?" asks Magda.

"Anything," says Nona, "Good meant blah, and I got so used to being surface-good that surface became substance, ME, as if feigned blah's ME all the way down, that's all there is."

"Only it really isn't, that's the problem. At the age of thirty-five ... oops, thirty-six, the flower's still in the process of defining itself as fruit. And then suddenly Bernadette comes along already small, but formed, like a six week foetus, or one of those little lime-buttons you fingernail into, and the air's full of flowers ... " says Magda.

"So it's my fault is it?" asks Bernadette, sad, Magda, as always very sadistically and purposefully pulling all the wrong triggers, pushing the wrong buttons, opening the wrong doors.

"In a way. Mimicry. Getting into the contextual swim ... "

"And me?"

Sadder all the time, and when she gets sadder she evolves/ages, the Earth becomes old with its life burden, you come up through the layers of the Olduvai Gorge from rich, heavy oozes into smaller, smarter (cunning) sadder bones and faces, consciousness become curse, you leave the Garden, you 'surface' and your complicated eyes stare out at the wind-devil emptiness of total desert.

"Your move," says Magda.

"Your ... ?"

"A senhora sabe/Her ladyship knows ... "

"Well, out of the nine, I'm the one between four and six, the fifth and the sixth. Well, Luiz is sixth. He always says 'I'm out-side ... totally, and he is, which is its own kind of Eden, and Paulo, Tereza, the others, they're so far 'in' that they're almost out on the other side. I mean they were 'moulded' so closely on parent-models that the models became them. They have this strong sense of self, belonging. And me ... you're not really dumped, not really actively ignored, you're just there, transparent, permanent, like walls and ceiling ... or – more recently – floor. The older ones escape into their 'older' identities. The younger ones plummage out into their own forests, but the unmarried fifth one who's always just 'around' ... see, I go back now expecting them to see me. I mean I'm different. My mother's dying somehow defined me. By becoming surrogate I became a ME, and it was an agreed-upon ME that I didn't like ... "

"Although," interrupts Magda, "let's say that you didn't mind/don't mind being you. Even you as Shadow of the Mother – and I see that in you, the rebirth of her in you – only real, not ersatz ... "

"Er ... ?"

"Fake. Sintetica. Não quer ser a mulher substituta de seu pai ... nem a mãe substituta para os seus irmãos ... you don't want to be the wife-substitute for your father, nor the mother substitute for your brothers and sisters. But you want to be a rebirth of your mother in you in the same type of liberation-context that she was HER in the first place. Although maybe without the negative factor that your father (the man) was in her life ... "

"The new, perfect model, with all the kinks out," smiles Bernadette, happier now, able to sink back a little out of twitchiness into sensual megaooze, massaging Madga's thighs, hands around her waist, "You're getting so thin ... real ribs and ... breast-bone ... "

"And me?" asks Nona, "me ... ?"

"God," thinks Magda, looking at her, heavily sad, the burden of the world/millennia/consciousness on her broad white shoulders, corroding inside her magnificent white skin, "it's happened again ... her destiny ... and Blah spoke unto Blah across the megacosmic vastness and Blah answered Blah with Blah, Blah echoing through the emptiness of Blah, and Blah said 'I am,' and the Blackness answered 'Nevermore ... not Am but Becoming ... ,' becoming and becoming and becoming, and fear comes in as the leaves etch across the paradisal spring and juice begins to define itself, take on skin and seeds ... fear-resentment ... 'How can I? How can I?' and Blah answers 'Nevermore.'"

"You're fine," says Magda, "Tudo bem!"

"Tudo bem!" answers Nona, Brazilian thumb-up, her thumb with this curse of a wart on it. Bernadette's been 'burning' it with nitric acid, cutting it, burning, cutting, but it keeps coming back, these little black seeds in the cakelike white thumbskin (nail off three different times), "Tudo bem, tudo bem, tudo bem … "

### xlviii.

Nona, Magda and Bernadette at the beginning of their almond-oiled back-rubbing yogic night, the kids in the other room watching a special on Luiz Peixoto's Brazil sambaing slowly toward the twenty-first century with lots of fin-de-siècle gold-dust still clinging to its romantic mulata surface. The kids don't speak English at all any more, even among themselves. Margaret forgets laranja is "orange," and Nona says "Get the scissors off the desk" and Alexandra doesn't know either "scissors" or "desk."

Maybe it's even worse (better) with Bernadette living there full time now. Magda never speaking English, slowly filing off the final corners of her Spanish to Portuguese transition. The only one hanging on to English Nona herself, and even she's 'eroding,' will say things like "Is there any 'rope' upstairs?" meaning roupa-clothes … and now that school's over they've turned into full-time TV-addicts. It pours into them all day and all evening, they go to bed at one or two and get up at eleven and watch the daytime serials/novelas, all about Paloma up in the air in her plane waiting for the gas to run out before she suicide-falls, and André fighting/loving Karina (in *Pai Heróe/Father Hero*). They all seem to be artificially 'hurried,' all the serials do, as if the writers have been told "You've got two more weeks to end the fucker." *Marrón Glacé* and *Água Viva/Live Water*, *Carinhosa/Loving*, *O Todo Poderoso/The All-Powerful*, the main thing they see is love inside the Brazilian disappearing-Cruzeiro economy, this have-everything beauticianed, bejewelled servant-surrounded middle class slowly suffocating with all the money-air cut off. "Bota água no feijão/Water down the beans," the whole key to the Brazilian economy.

When Magda asks Margaret what makes the difference between a great novela and a pipsqueak, she says "Em uma boa a gente pode sentir o que está acontecendo está verdadeiramente acontecendo … se não vale e porque a gente sente que os atores estão só representando/If it's good you can feel what's happening is really happening … and if it's not worth anything it's because you feel that the actors are only acting."

There had been a big love-affair with the neighbour-kids, but they came at 9 am, left at 9 pm, broke lots of toys, and Nona would get really pissed off. "I don't care how protein-starved they are, they ate twelve little yoghurts in one afternoon. It's not the money, but who wants to go to the store every day!"

Finally everyone got lice and Donna Betty, Katia's and Simone's mother, got pissed off and said categorically they didn't and wouldn't use medicine on them, and the War of the Lice began, Katia finally ringing the doorbell one night and asking Magda if she can talk to Alexandra. Alexandra comes to the door.

"Did you say I have lice?"

"Well, you do."

And she slaps Alex across the face. That's it, the gate closes and the house (psyche) folds back in on itself.

*O Sitio de Picopau Amarelo/The Place of the Yellow Woodpecker* is their favourite, this magic place (sitio) in the country inhabited by Emilia, the ragdoll, Visconde, the corncob doll, the mythological one-legged black-boy, Sací, who can appear and disappear at will, Donna Benta, the grandmother, talking trees, trips to the moon, trips into other books and stories like Don Quixote or Aladdin's magic-lamp world. It's a tropical, green, rural-jungle sentient flowering world of blacks, whites, ducks, forest … and all possibility …

That's their favourite. And *Charlie's Angels* and *Wonder Woman*.

*Pai Herói.*

Watch Margaret's face when Karina and André fall kissing into bed.

"You'd think she'd just react to women," says Nona one day, "I mean, you know, us and all … "

"The Gay World emerges from the 'normal' middle class, you know that … "

Beach-season begins. They start going to the almost legendary Praie do Forte. You stand up in the eighteenth century fort itself and you can see the enemy sails approach the island, there's a visual command of wide, wide seas, and then down to the empty beach that the Argentinians don't seem to have discovered yet. There's these shallows that reach way out into the sea, the sails of flat waves that sweep in softly feathered, topped by delicious bubbly foam. And you look back, up at the hills and it's all bananas and palms. It's *O Sitio de Picapau Amarelo/The Place of the Yellow Woodpecker* transposed off the TV into flesh and foam. Even the house … you look out the back verandah and it's bananas and eucalyptus and palms. You can understand how the first scurvy-dying sailors walking into the perpetual monkey-orange-palm green thought that they'd rediscovered Eden.

"But what kind of influence will all this have on them?" asks Nona.

"*Lord Jim*, I keep thinking *Lord Jim*. Joseph Conrad. I can smell the incense and hear the tam-tams … I'm not quite Balinese Gamelan monkey-dances, my idiom is still western, but my sensibilities are pure East, I never really sail north of the Tropic of Cancer," answers Magda.

## xlix.

Grades all handed in. Summer-Christmas flying all its wild flags.

Magda walking by the magazine kiosk and the bookstore at the university, all these new poured-concrete buildings, and the poor still sliding down from the hills every time it rains, you'd think the government would …

Thinking of piles of dead days and piles of shit, starving pelicans coming into Lima and they'd run into them with cars, kill them with sticks, black asphalt stained with bright red blood. You'd think the government could …

Past the stand of eucalyptus next to the gym/swimming pool, and suddenly she's in Ollantaytambo, the long rows of eucalyptus and the innocently clear Andean riachuelos/streams feeding the beginnings of the Amazon. Across the street, up past the houses of the poor, Katia's grandfather, "Boa tarde/Good afternoon," folkloric old man, you feel that in his head, behind his Buddha-St. Francis face, he is the Wisdom of the Tribe.

Donna Betty outside in a bathrobe. She's just had an abortion. Kids talk.

"Tudo bem?/Everything OK?" asks Magda.

"Melhorando./Getting better."

As if she were just getting over a cold.

She's all puffy and you can see her face passing from girl to old lady …

Then she's at the iron gates of her own place, opens them, and there's the big brick (German) house and behind it the swirl of jungle green. The screen-door is closed, she rings the bell and Sonia opens it. She has on an ecru cotton dress from Ceará that Magda gave her for her birthday. Her hair is all carefully combed and she has on coffee-coloured lipstick.

"Usé um pouco de seu esmalte./I used a little of your fingernail polish. OK?"

"OK … " and Magda imagines her in bed, mulata sinewy-boney intensity, the long-distance endurance of the woman (19), like when she sweeps outside she goes on for half an hour. Like a machine. Imagine that machine pumping into Antonio. Or into her.

"Tudo pronto para café./Coffee's ready. Eu vou embora./I'm going to go now … "

Sun mostly gone now, rusty whore-light dusted over the green, the bats coming out now, the nocturnal world of cats, snakes, bats, spiders, dogs, mosquitos beginning to come alive.

"I wish I could begin my day at dusk," Magda says.

"You're finished today. You can, can't you?"

"I've got the surgery coming up, but then … I'm starting to get jowls/queixadas) … "

"Mas não dá para ver … you can't see them … "

"I can."

Fingering into the falling face, thinking, no, I wouldn't have cared if there were multiple lives involved and I could just enjoy the beauty of this particular beautiful face aging, but …

"Bom/Good … " getting her bags together, purse, Magda going into her purse, handing her ten Cruzeiros for carfare.

"Até segunda, então/See you on Monday, then," calling back into the house, "Tchau/So long," Nona's and Bernadette's voices echoing back "Tchau," Magda and Sonia kiss, one cheek, then the other. Magda can smell her perfume (Dernier Cri) on Sonia.

Then Sonia's gone and Magda latches the screen, comes in and kisses Bernadette and Nona. They're in Bernadette's room making these purses out of very Japanese-looking gold and red (chrysanthemum?) cloth.

"Beautiful … "

"Rio's waiting for us. You've got to think up a label."

"The Last Word," says Magda, "Dernier-Cri … "

"Not bad," says Nona.

"Let me think about it a while," she says and goes in, kisses the kids (sitting watching *Picapau Amarelo*), into the bathroom, her flowered chiffon sticking to her skin as she takes it off. Bothered by her sagging breasts and belly. Does she really believe, short of the Second Coming, that you can actually (pulls in her gut, blows out a little air) reverse time?

Not exactly, but still, you can keep it all as long as you can, even improve on what you already had (have).

She almost feels like eating the Jaruá (honey and turtle-lard) soap with its sweet brown-sugary smell.

Into the shower, washing away the day, washing away John Derrick and Mike Jayne, washing away Carmen Rosa and Hilario Bohn, washing away catalogues, meetings, terror, studied sadism, institutions as sado-masochistic games, the would-be artists and saints who never quite made it, gathered around the round table feeling her (the Magna Mater) a threat, at the same time (bode expiatório/expiatory offering) a victim. Only I'm Medea," she says out loud and for a moment becomes a fiery dragon, then suddenly turns into "Little girl hurt," hit, tied, locked up, starved, God love the Irish and the Good Sisters and their knuckle-whipping birch-rods. The human itself is so sick. The animals neither weep nor anguish for their sins. Loves the spume in her hair and across her body. Vampirella. Take Two …

Then out, drying with a big fluffy white towel that smells like it's just been ironed, rubs some clove-sharp copaiba oil on her legs where she's (heat) getting all these little infected hair-follicles.

It's such an emblematic world. It's all there (like anti-diarrhoea Goiaba tea) just waiting to be discovered. Blow-dries her hair, wishes it was thicker, more of a mane, pulls on her new black-lace-breasted camisole, black stockings, transparent plastic slip-into heels, dark out now, except for a yellow split in the western black clouds. Almost crying with joy she closes the iron gates on the lost, sick Out There and comes back into the house, her black thighs just waiting, waiting, waiting to open on the sanity of their shared Night.

## 1.

It's so perfect when Christmas vacation and summer come together.

"Imagine, I've never been to Lima in summer," says Magda over breakfast, late (10:30) and they wouldn't get up before noon if Sonia didn't come and ring the bell.

"Imagine, I've never been there at all," says Bernadette.

"And I don't wanna go at all," smirks Nona.

Sonia sitting there mouse-eyed. She sits at the table with them now during meals. But it's forma de costume/outside the usual thing, so she's uncomfortable.

"This funny dream about my father … "

Magda's supposed to be, they're all supposed to be eating this health food place's (VIDA) whole wheat bread-cake, but they're all eating rolls from the local venda/store, Magda lots of butter, fig jelly ("I'm not going to skimp on breakfast, if I don't eat another thing all day … ") the thinness showing now, in unexpected places like the upper arms, "I dreamt about my father, he had this funny kind of hinged chest and you could open it up, it was like a luggage compartment inside, all the organs neatly enclosed in plastic. And I crept inside and started to cry and say 'I love you so much, my sweet father … '"

Embarrassed, another little buttered-jammed scrap of crust.

"You wanted him to be a mother," Nona says, "It's a luggage compartment womb, you want to crawl back into the paternal womb … "

"I dreamed there was this fat black man after me, you know this blonde guy I've got a crush on … ? His wife at the window helped me get out/away," says Sonia, loving to talk, tell stories.

"Your step-father?" asks Magda, thinking thirteen 'stepfathers,' and the only one her mother married was the last, her last.

That's what Sonia always says, her mother is a black leathery lizardish sag-bag of a cleaning woman, over, but over/out/kaput at, what, forty, forty-two …

"Maybe … he's after me, you know, only my mother would kill me if I'd ever do anything with him (si desse bola a ele) … "

"And you've never loved a man?" asks Magda. Feeling very, very close to her, no distance at all.

"I like," says Sonia, "I appreciate, but love … ? The only one I've ever really loved in my life is my mother."

"You don't love your husband?" asks Bernadette.

"No … not love … I sometimes even enjoy sex, but … and then I think back, I was, what, eleven, when I first met him, he was a friend of my brothers, and I'd go around topless because I had nothing on top, these short shorts, I'd drag my arse on the ground, legs up in front of him. I wanted him between my legs, with my chain around his neck … I don't know … " stops, laughs, a two months pregnant brown paper bag of bones.

"You know, Donna Maggi," she says later (doing the dishes), working up to a Statement (which Magda would just as soon avoid), "I can't get used to the other one around … "

"Bernadette?"

Looking Magda cynically-defiantly in the eye.

"Do you really make 'love' together?"

"We take turns, never the three together. I wouldn't mind, but Bernadette – mainly – doesn't want it that way."

Disgust, almost anger on Sonia's face.

"Sabe, que eu não consigo nem imaginar como deve ser./I can't even imagine how it must be."

"It's softer, that's one thing it is, softer, longer. It hangs on, there's no hurry. It's visual, it's incense in the air, all the same texture … "

"And you use … ?" hand to her mouth.

"Sometimes. Don't you and Antonio?"

"Credo!/Never!"

"I look at you," says Magda, "listen to you, and I understand why there's never been a revolution in Brazil. I mean never."

"Como?/What?"

Hooked now. Curious.

"Because a revolution isn't 'routine,' and for you … isn't routine, maybe that's not the word, 'the customary,' the already-done, the 'traditional' … I mean, revolution would be a thing to be ashamed of."

"Não sei … I don't know … " hands with nails coming off, all of the nails swollen around the bases, allergic to the brown laundry soap she's washing the dishes in, with detergent (Mago-Limão) in a plastic bottle right in front of her that she's not allergic to but won't use.

"Because I can't afford it at home," she says, and Magda won't say "But you're here now, you're not at home … "

Eyeing them all as day progresses to night, the centre of their velvet world, as purple and beige turn black, hair gets washed and faces and eyes theatricalised, the camisoles begin to appear, flesh takes on the flavour of sugar and spice … and she begins to get hungry for it.

TV on, a re-run of *O Casarão*. About an old-man painter and an old-woman just-widow who come together again excruciatingly after being forty years apart.

Magda feels the calm, steady, time-flow.

The image of a Brazilian movie she saw in the US comes into her mind, another 40 year separation, the man returns, out of the city back to the Sertão/Outback, time stops in the dusk afterglow under outback-hot still palms.

Stepping through the time-wall, disintegrating.

Later there's the film version of *Justine*.

The images almost make it, the sound is Hollywood Mid-East, there's this one death-bed scene that almost makes it, a final last question that gets to her, "Everyone ends up here, don't they?"

Nona unmoving on the bed, inert, sleeping, her hand on Magda's legs. Magda wants to tell her, "Wake up and watch, you're missing … " remembering when they read *The Alexandria Quartet* on FM all night in Boston, loved the books.

Anouk Aimée didn't make it (too smooth, too French) as Justine, the almost-biblical whore. She can't be that smooth to be real.

Midnight and the kids still up. Alexandra gets herself a bottle. The TV's in their room and they're watching *Justine* too. At one Magda goes in there and they're asleep. She covers them and Nona gets up.

"I'm going to leave you two alone … " heavy in Magda's arms, thirty-five but with the flaccidity of ninety, like a sack of beans, coffee, flour.

"Are you OK?"

"Tired … "

Magda walks her down to the bedroom with the kids, holds her. It's like carrying a side of beef into bed. Magda goes back to Bernadette and lights the dracula red candle. They're all bat black, start to lizard-kiss, massive and delicate black legs intertwine, Bernadette's small perfect breasts, Magda's anxious tongue, daggered fingers around Bernadette's thighs, anus-vagina, the Beatitude Membrane between the two, Bernadette all wet, Magda going through the motions, only then she becomes an eye looking down at them from the ceiling, looking at herself, the sagging blonde moonface and the (recently) frizzed recently blonde hair, her belly … she'd never really "come back" since her last child, twenty years before.

"Can I 'come back' to what I was?" she'd asked Bernadette, the Yoga Mistress.

"You can. If you contract your stomach muscles a thousand times a day like a clenched fist. It's all WILL!"

But the sag stays on in spite of all her clenchings and under all the blonde she knows, doesn't she, that this professor-whore's a REJECT next to Bernadette's bed-dancer perfection.

And hearses drag themselves through the room in the midst of her love-making, black horses with black plumes on their foreheads, hoarse, windy voices whispering around her ears, "You didn't stop and wait for Death, so Death has stopped and waited for you." The horses' heads aimed at eternity. Only they're not there for her, are they, but …

Magda stops altogether.

"What's wrong?"

"I'm not 'here,'" answers Magda, "She's only thirty-five … "

"Não estou entendendo/I don't understand."

"Let's go and take a look at her."

Up and into the big bedroom, Nona lying there face all flushed, eyes open, laboriously, lugubriously drawing in breath.

"Oh, for crissake … " and Magda goes into the bathroom for the bronchodilator (Bricanyl) spray.

"Here, use this."

"It makes me shake."

"For crissake, use it. If you don't you won't have to worry about shaking, that's for sure."

Nona reluctantly putting it to her mouth, spraying, dragging in, holding, letting it circulate, the whole time Nona's fingers kneading her chest, lower sternum, diaphragm.

"What's that all about?" Magda asks.

"It hurts."

"Heart?" Magda asks Bernadette, and Bernadette shakes her head. What does she know, she's a surgeon.

Magda gets the bottle of Pulmol out of the bathroom. Nona wants a spoon.

"Swig it, for crissake, swig it!"

But she won't. Bernadette gets a spoon and she takes her spoonful.

And then the wait begins, they sit there while Nona labours, claws at her chest.

"Get on your side," says Magda.

"It's uncomfortable," objects Nona.

"It's a little late for that now," says Bernadette.

"She hasn't been coughing at all for the last couple of days. Coughing. Coughing up. She doesn't take the medicine, and with the amount of fruit she doesn't eat every day, I don't know how she doesn't end up with scurvy."

"Como?"

"Escorobuto ... I mean people die even in Brazil ... " then to Nona, "How do you feel?"

"Better."

Lungs like dry organ-bellows, leather soles shuffling on summer sidewalks, sandpaper lungs, plastic garbage-bag lungs, old yellowed newspaper pages crumbling when you try to turn them ...

"Should we call an ambulance?" Magda asks Bernadette, Bernadette sitting there afraid, that's what it is, isn't it, afraid, her mother died of this same kind of intractable asthma, "No lungs left," she always says, her mother's come for a visit, hasn't she, is hovering there in the darkness, re-breathing her last breaths ...

(I couldn't stop and wait for Death ... )

"I don't know."

The game of All the Answers that Bernadette refuses to play. Margaret wakes up, then Alexandra. They huddle around Nona, faces heavy, drawn ... but it's too soon, they know that ... too soon for her to 'leave' ... Magda thinking back, Michigan, Buenos Aires, those terrible chest colds, the accumulation of scar-tissue, and no sense of general health infra-structure ...

The sexuality of Black's cancelled out, you can smell Death in the room, it's all white, the neuter sexlessness of beyond death, grey ash (Wednesday) ... as somewhere around dawn, when the wild chickens begin to cluck and claw outside, Nona begins to breathe almost normally.


**li.**

The movie's *The Man in the Grey Flannel Suit.* Magda feels she ought to watch it. Gregory Peck, Jennifer Jones, the history of film/culture and all that.

Only it's too real, the image of the trapped neurotic, the money-centred (money as love-substitute) suburban hausfrau is her ... or maybe she's him, passive little slave/hack, the unsure-of-herself workslave.

1:30. They're all three on the bed, the red satin (a little too theatrical?) sheets, Nona's been out (you get used to her as asthma zombie), now she stirs.

It's Bernadette's night with Magda anyhow.

Bernadette's ready, black crotchless stockings and all lace camisole, purple eyelids and lips. What's changing – her, or Magda's perception of her – or both? From skinny runt to sex-dagger, she's all mucosal now.

Lips, nipple-knobs/-bulbs, her (their) legs becoming shimmering black, zipper-squeaking clitoral tongues.

Not interested in "climax," that irritating tea-time word, buttered, honey, figjam, banana, bread-cake, gostoso (delicious) her exclusive candlelit vocabulary, interested in the passage, not the arrival.

"I'm going to bed," says Nona.

"And I've had enough grey flannel suits," says Magda, eye-asking Bernadette "OK?" "OK," turning off the TV, Nona kissing them, maybe she'd like to stay but Bernadette wants it pairs, not threesomes, "When there's three, the victim/victimized equilibrium's upset ... " she'd said more than once, which said all there was to say about her concept of love/love-relationships.

And with unstraight Nona there's always shame, under all her craziness the doric-columned, midwest Methodist-Congregationalist "censor" is always there wondering why Nona is involved with women at all.

With sagging Slavic Magda it's not shame that bothers her, but an all-embracing sense of decay, decline, death ...

"See you later."

The door closes and Magda lights the blood red love-candle, a tiny piece of sandalwood stick, thinking that all their love-making should be done soaked in musk-oil on rubber sheets, in, under oil.

The great enemy is MIND thinks Magda as the Ritual of Tongues begins. And suddenly John Derrick's there, squinting through his Berkeley-Buddha glasses.

"You can't stay another year ... you're not one of us."

And then Magda's in the final histology exam in med school, tables covered with microscopes all around the walls, you get three minutes per slide, identify, move on, Magda takes a glance, 2, 3 seconds, she knows they've stuck in a bunch of pathological specimens, they always fuck you over as much as they can ... one, two, write, looks around at the others, white cotton instead of grey flannel, the one other woman in the class is a ski-slide nosed loser, although she has nice (soft) legs ... Magda wants OUT, the tension's building, why is she taking final exams when she doesn't even want to be there ... ?

"What's wrong?" asks Bernadette.

"What ... ?"

And she's back in the flickering red Siva-temple glow, Bernadette's kneading her arms.

"You're cataleptic."

"I'm sorry," pleading with herself, cOMe, cOMe, cOMe into the hOMe sweet NOW, but she doesn't get there.

Her mother talking now.

"You're out of the will until you come back into decency and normality. You killed your father, but I'm not going to let you kill me ... "

"What's the difference who or how I love, what's the difference to you?" and she streams into, flows into tears.

"What's going on?"

"I don't know. The university ... Derrick ... you know I flunked out of medical school, I didn't walk out, I flunked out ... "

Bernadette the Great Mother, comforting. It's all to do with There/the US, the system there, even (*The Man in the Grey Flannel Suit*) diluted dubbed-in TV contact with There does it.

"Sometimes you'd just like to be 'normal', wouldn't you, I mean a doctor's wife conformista/conformist ... wouldn't you?" asks Bernadette.

"Not really ... all I want is to be HERE, I don't want my head in 1950 ... it's gone, and before Now goes I want to simply BE ... "

"You ought to do yoga with me and Nona every night, yoga and diet and ... "

"A little plastic face-work ... ?"

"OK."

"Give me a chance to recoup some of the M.D.-Ph.D. years I lost ... "

"Smell," says Bernadette, "breathe in, you're at the centre of your forehead, moving up to the top of your head ... see, feel it bloom ... "

Warmth, like warm fudge between Magda's legs and her tongue moves out to Bernadette's nipples like a glistening, trembling pink finger.


## lii.

Magda to Bernadette.

"Of course we'll go to Nona's parents first. I mean you two will. I'll have to go out and visit my mother. My penance for the year. She's seventy-five now, I don't really want to see her. Or I want to see her, but not HER. I want to get off the plane and there's another her waiting for me. The last scene in *The Four-Poster*, all the old podre/rotten relations buried and then re-sprouting, celestial seeds, see the old lady glowing there in her mink stole and hat, my dearly beloved daughter, unconditionally welcome, instead of the reality of 'What in the world have you done with your hair ... apart from the fact that those heels are destroying your whole pelvic area, you look like you a you-know-what ... I'm ashamed to show you to anybody. In fact to even be seen with you.' And then I'd like to go to San Francisco and visit Richard Morris for a couple of days, just long enough to not wear out my welcome, and I'll meet you two back in Michigan, early September, it hardly seems like 'Autumn' at all at first, in a sense is summer intensified, summer juiced-up, dried-out, a yellower, richer, heavier summer, and in a sense that's what it is, summer going to flower, seed, harvest, the temperature goes down slowly, the nights become cold, bald, white old men dreaming dreams of death, cadaverous old men who won't lie down, caps and wool coats on cadaver bodies awkwardly walking through the nights and peering inside windows at the dead sleepers. The leaves get crisp and red and yellow and start to fall, the air's perfumed with resins, and then it begins to rain, the leaves strip off, the colour goes, Old Man Night lies down and the first snows try to cover him, don't make it, the ground has to get cold too, but it does, and then it's over, it's shrouds for … five months … of course we'll go down to Kansas City for Christmas, just after Christmas, that's when I go crazy, there's all these sales, especially on shoes … all the big sizes you can dream of … and clothes … we should get you pregnant as soon as you can, in fact maybe you ought to get pregnant down here, someone you (genetically) know … choose what you want, you've got the family context, you can figure out more or less exactly what you're getting, you have the child up there, and then you're the mother of an American citizen. And East Ford, you'll love it, college town, really nothing else. I was just talking to Margaret the other day, she wants to study ballet. OK, the ballet studio's two blocks away. She wants to study guitar. OK, I get a music student to come over to the house, we're three blocks away from the music school. We've got our own university TV station, our own FM station that's like the Ministry of Education and Culture's station in Rio and Brasilia … you name it, we've got it, we'll have to get the living room redone, I mean entirely. I want a luxurious relax-room, not just a somewhere but PARADISO … all pillows, sandalwood, ginseng and … pleasure … you know your body is perfect. That's the way I'm really beginning to see you, as perfect, like something out of a pornographic comic strip, Vampirella, something like that. We really ought to design a line of fun-clothes around that idea. What do you think, huh?"

She looks down at her stretched out naked on the bed, head cradled on Magda's lap.

Doesn't answer. Of course she's out. Sound asleep, and Magda wonders (dream of Old Man Winter) for how long:

It's raining, it's pouring,
the old man is snoring …
it's snowing, it's blowing,
the old man is …

Closes her eyes. The Hibernation Factor. This sudden – is she all right, she wonders – sweep of cansaço/fatigue …

### liii.

Magda a week in the Dracula-house in the congealed emerald garden alone, every night she'd lock all the doors that led to this central passage, the heavy wooden shutters on her window, locked the window, the doors.

And still noise-shapes would amorphously move through the boogie-night, slither their scales against her window and breathe heavy against the cracks around the doors ... hungry adversary rapist god, Lord of Cobras and Cats ...

Nona, Bernadette and the kids in São Paulo to get Nona's nose operated on.

"Well, without the nose as filter ... once it's opened I'm sure her whole asthma problem will, if not disappear, then certainly be improved (vai melhorar)," Doctor Costa had said, but wasn't willing to operate.

São Paulo versus Florianópolis, like Yankton, South (or is it North?) Dakota versus Manhattan.

"There's this mini-trauma micro-surgical technique they use," Bernadette had said.

Looked at Nona, lard-body, sloth, sleepwalker, woman in walking-dead white, warm cadaver cooling, still soft on the edge of death-hard, thirty-six, the Dozer, Haunter, puffy rubber-doll woman.

Hold her up and she (barely) opens her eyes.

"Imprescindível/It's something that has to be done," said Bernadette, "tem que ir ... you have to go," so they went to Tereza's (Bernadette's sister's) place in São Paulo, and Magda stayed home, on the edge of finals, two dissertation defences (bancas), it would have been "hardship" for her to leave now, especially trying to keep the peace with Machão Hilario ...

Paranoid, pop-eyed Night growls outside.

She's all in black, in front of the mirror, too Slavic-jawed, too old, and she oughta wash her hair every day with Wella Balsam dye-shampoo, but ...

She still comes off as fleshpot, that depraved pleasure-giver (taker) look about her, ecstatic, sybarite, houri, Mahatma pleasure-angels carrying her up to Mogul gardens of heavenly delights ...

But the old Narcissism doesn't work, her-flesh doesn't respond to her-flesh in a her-self vacuum anymore, made up and black tourmaline-earringed, negligéed and black-legged, she longs for a VICTIM ...

A week later and they're back, Nona's nose new, her flesh almond-paste sweet, swollen but breathing, thin, tubercular Wings of the Dove delicious. Only it's Bernadette's "turn" first.

She amazed, as they begin, winged Hermes-snake black-legs intertwined, amazed she's so THERE, the clarity of There, the clarity of Bernadette's thighs and the fat of her underlegs (gastrocnemius), the clarity of her own lightning pinstuck pleasure-stabs, breathing in the night desperately, a smile across the face of chakra serpent-pelvis clarity.

This is the "how" of her last years, the retreat-retirement into the mountains of Self (shared). They will create their own London, the Out There will wane and die, and the membranes of self grow and fill the organ-cavities of night ...

Later on, emptying the garbage, it's full of maggots. Bernadette recoils from them, Magda lets them crawl all over her hands, thrusts into their fermenting, twisting warmth, glorying in the smell of the garbage, shit, fermented, sweet-bitter, the esters of decay, remembering back in Michigan the maggots in garbage in a closed back-porch, and she left them alone out there and within days the room was filled with hundreds of Lord of the Flies gods ...

### liv.

Standing in front of the mirror all pink-blonde (wig) fluffy, mesh legs and (bra-less) black lace camisole.

"It's so wonderful to have a body ... "

Pulling in her gut as Nona comes in.

"I'm ashamed, but let me say it. Epitaph: AT LEAST BEFORE SHE DIED SHE FELT – EVEN IF IT WAS FOR A VERY SHORT TIME – WHAT IT WAS TO BE A CUTESY-POOH."

The words belying the reality, as a mute roar of genetic fulfilment descends on her hot, slim rose-skinned form and she becomes a lizard emerging out of slime, out of the egg, the womb, wet with birth, as all the secret purposes inside her converge on an emphatic overridingly sensuous I AM ME.

Nona comes over.

"And what's this ... "

"Raspberry."

Nipples. Nona begins to suck and the room girates, all the angles obliquely awkward, tumbling in the purple-rose-pineapple ceiling-light, Nona's face above her grinning (Gotcha now), the triumphal warmth of being a successful fire-starting whore ... the lids close ... out ...

### lv.

Magda straps herself into corset (with the breasts cut out), black stockings, garter belt, black dagger-heel boots.

"I don't like it," says Bernadette.

"Well, it does kind of look like it was made by Gillette," says Magda, fingering the sharp-edged metal garters.

"You know who always wore/wears garter belts," says Nona, "My sister Jean … "

And Jean's suddenly THERE, 'wet' between Magda's legs, Jean of the afternoon camisole nylon across nylon draped creamy legs, ruffle-Jean, fringe-Jean, hair almost over her eyes, ashamed-Jean, ashamed of her own imaginings, ashamed, afraid …

"I tell you what I like about turn-of-the-century New Orleans whorehouses," says Magda, "they're all skin-existentialism, flesh-deductive … "

And she's flooded with low flesh-lights, the hour of flasked, satined, soft-gartered, smoothed, massaged, curled, slippery, spongy Preparation, and the Hours of Submissive, Un-Thought, All-Feel, gliding, deep-breathing, surrendering, defeated-victorious Debussyian satori …


**lvi.**

Laying back in the jasmine-incensed night, Bernadette never really stops, the rubbing, petting, 'consoling' goes on, first inside the uterine aquarium, and then up along all the gullies and runnels of ecstasy …

"Nunca tem o suficiente, não é … ?/There never is enough, is there?" says Magda.

"Acho que não/I guess not … "

Magda watching the incense-snakes writhe up into the candlelight, thinking there must have been a golden age of Brahmas in India, it couldn't all be as wife-selling and buying (and suffering) as now, all reduced to the Good (Barter) Marriage, the hermaphroditic Siva statue she'd left back in Michigan dancing in her mind, "Golden Age, Golden Age … "

Catching a glimpse of herself in the mirror, the face becoming box, becoming Prague, the Slavic nations, a jowled, jewelled dumpling.

"You are going to re-do my face, aren't you?"

Bernadette dismissing her with "Sure, sure … "

"No, really!"

"You want me to get up right now and check my appointment book?"

Magda angry, everything she ever wants always getting put off, the anti-god tridenting-wielding Siva angrily emerging out of her computerised, fluorescent-ceilinged head …

"Later … "

And Magda reaches her fleshy black-nyloned toe up Bernadette's black thigh, Bernadette winces, wounded, weakened as she pushes her toe into Bernadette's groin. Magda with these educated feet that talk to Bernadette's groin.

Bernadette's legs expanding, both of their legs expanding, turning from legs to coils, scale-slithering-clicking along each other, filling the room, rubbing glistening against the wet mucous walls, closing tighter and tighter around each other until their red mouths open and their red tongues touch and python around each other until they can hardly breathe, everything gostoso/delicious, their ecstasies hissing through the moist, spring night room as love becomes a dancing of mating scorpions, crabs, mucous-sheathed worms on wet dawn grass ...

Then afterwards Magda talking to Bernadette, although she's not sure if she's even awake:

"I don't want to die slowly. I mean when I do die, I don't want to face it slowly like peeling an artichoke, becoming less and less inside the awareness that I'm really becoming nothing at all. I can't stand the idea of consciously unravelling and dissolving. Or being like Hubert Humphrey, you hang on, become transparent, all tubes and sacks, and the bichos/bugs are still inside you like termites in an old house ... you know, being gay, you're outside, crazy ... and you see it more fully ... visão global/global vision ... I mean I never for a moment think that exercise or diet or surgery are going to make any real difference ... the only reality is the diss–olving ... like I used to know this Israeli woman in Caracas, you know, the perfect coordinated-colour type, shoes, dress, nails, lipstick, this haystack of brittle blonde hair, and she never was pretty, her parents were from Poland, I think, originally ... these coarse features ... that was fourteen years ago, she must have been, what, 35, 36 then ... she's in her fifties, I suppose, another ten years ... it's such a short time ... it's already 2050 and I've been dead for ... you know what my head just did, made me fifty in 2000, made me thirty instead of fifty now ... I mean to think that in twenty years I'll be seventy ... I'll be like all my mother's old-folks friends, and they must feel like me, I mean it just happened to them the way it happened to me, and we really stayed twenty, twenty-five inside, that never really changed ... I mean no one ever really feels old, do they?"

Bernadette asleep, Magda looks down at her anaconda leg-coils, anaconda, eternal Ananta, Krishna-her stretched out on the leg-coils of eternity, dreaming the dream called existence, afraid to wake up and pop it all like a (Homage to Carmen Miranda) balloon.

lvii.

The night before Magda's operation, the unscheduled-scheduled unspoken flow of nights, it's Bernadette's "turn" to be with Magda, but she doesn't costume into black lace, stays Indian-skirted, lilac-bloused, Chacrinha's (Tuesday) Amateur (Calouros) Hour on the TV, sound off as they wait for someone good to appear on the screen between the amateurs, which is maybe once or twice an evening … still, the Chacrettes compensate in their sequinned bathing suits and silver high-heeled boots.

Bernadette is making a violet purse, violet, lilac, purple. Nona thinks Lent. It's an Ash Wednesday Lenten mood when it should be the cock's crow of Advent.

"Let's make some coffee," Nona tells Bernadette, Magda sitting there all frizzed, frizzing some more in the mirror. If she frizzes enough, Nona thinks, she'll frizz out into a tumbleweed ball of split-ends, dandelion-fluff, shedding cattails, thistle-fluff, duck-down.

The minute Nona and Bernadette are in the kitchen the TV sound goes up.

"She'd listen to anything," says Nona, "see what a good influence we are on her … "

"A verdade, mas não estamos aqui só para fazer café, não e?/That may be true, but we're not just here to make coffee are we?"

"I've got a theory about your being down."

"Down?"

"Deprimida."

"Não estou, não … I'm not, really … "

"While the whole room sags … oh, my townspeople, let me show you how to make a funeral."

"Como fazer o que?/To do what?"

"You're worried about the surgery. You think something's going to go wrong. You're into post-death already, we're back in the States, the winters never end, what was between us was her … "

"O que estaval entre nós foil ela? Não penso assim, mas não posso negar que/What was between us was her? I don't think that way, but you can't deny that … "

The idiot Hulk sitting in there watching the idiot Hulk show.

"I never met anyone quite as, I don't know, I want to say 'shameless as a virtue,' at the same time super-self-conscious and unconscious of self. I want to say realistic, vulgar as in Vulgate, people/gente/povo, peasant, solid … I mean is she afraid?"

"Esta bem medrosa/she's very afraid. Very much so, more … than … "

"Than what?"

"Elle me disse que a diferença entre morrer agora e morrer em mais vinite/vinte e cinco anos, considerado dentre de vastidão do tempo en si, não é diferença nehuma … /she told me that the difference between dying now or in twenty or twenty-five more years, seen from the point of view of absolute time, isn't any difference at all … "

"But she's still afraid … "

"Afraid of 'dissolving', she says, like we have the impression we're solid, but what we are is gente de fumaça (smoke-people) gente de sal ou açúcar (salt- or sugar-people), and she, anyhow, says that she spent the first twenty years of her life being conditioned to expect a glorious resurrection, take that away and it's all dissolving, if she'd been conditioned to expect just that, no problem, but it's encher a mesa (fill the table) e após tirar tudo (afterwards take it all away) … if you'd been told from the beginning 'You're a being that dissolves', then when the end comes you wouldn't break down (desfazer-se em lágrimas) … the whole thrust (jeito) of life X is permanence, from time-payments on a houses to getting X fixed and buying Y next year or in two years … "

"But it's built-in, isn't it?"

"I don't think so. I think it's cultural conditioning … "

The hot water on now, Bernadette always puts it in the kettle hot from the tap, coffee in the filter, the mobilizing of fig and guava and strawberry jam, almond-blossom honey …

"But do you think she'll be OK?"

"Não sei, I don't know, but … "

"There's all these horror stories … like the woman last week who bled to death after a Caesarian, or the girl up in Pernambuco who had her tonsils out and something went wrong with the anaesthetic and she's in a permanent coma … "

"The more you know, the worse you know it is … or the better … I mean the statistics aren't that bad … and if you look at the body, I mean LOOK AT IT, you wonder how it works at all ever, not that there's a disease (malfunction) but health (function) … but to put me in the position of a clairvoyant (clarevidente) … I'm not, can't be … which is another WHY for getting out of Medicine, getting out of the role of being 'different', as if superior knowledge immunizes me against dissolving … facing my own death … you facing yours … if we were a Dissolving-Facing Civilisation instead of an Eternal Time-Payment one, we'd be a lot happier … "

Magda coming into the kitchen.

"What's the conspiracy?"

Nona looking at the frizz-ball cloud on top of Magda's head.

"My god, it looks like an atomic bomb."

"Anyone interested in a little atomizing tonight, the condemned woman's final fuck … "

"Not funny," says Nona, Nona down now, the Holy City of Garnet and Amethyst dissolving in her head.

"I'm interested," says Bernadette, OK now, although Death-thoughts never really left her, feelings of dissolving, on her back, eyes closed, a martyred saint at the moment of beatific immolation.

## lviii.

"Routine," which hides the face of the God-Jaguar under an expressionless masks of The Benign, Bernadette insisting to the end that she didn't want to do the surgery anyhow, not on the face of the Loved One, her Love, her Dove, her Beautiful One, "You don't really need it … "

"I get up in the mornings sometimes and I look at myself with loathing," says Magda.

"Loathing?"

"Asco in Spanish."

"Aborrecimento …" says Nona.

"Why?" Bernadette fingering around Magda's eyes and cheeks, the face plastically forming, unforming, re-forming, young, older, Slavic slanted eyes and then German heaviness, The Dumpling Eaters, and then the Irish Blythe Spirit.

"I'm not like her," she said pointing to Nona, Nona's beastly feet on Magda's lap, "in the anteroom of The Eternal. I'm just here, clay, grey, getting greyer … "

"I like character in a face," says Nona.

"And when I get enough 'character' you'll both drop me, unless you can get turned on by the ashes of last week's newspaper."

Especially, she thought, when you look from below and see the full smack of the frog-neck and jaw. From the side it looks like a rubber ball with a hooknose stuck on it.

"Of course I'm afraid … it's normal … "

"Of what?" Bernadette a little piqued. Besides she does love the aging flesh and she knows Nona does too. How much has she talked about the sweetness of her grandmother's ninety-three-year-old flesh just before she died, milk and honey flesh, milk and strawberries, and her own mother, love having nothing to do with …

"All three of us in this room are going to have a last moment, just like the babies, they'll have a last moment."

Bernadette tenses.

"I hate to even think about it."

"But it's there. Nothing inside of Nothing inside of Nothing … I hate it."

"If you're older you don't hate it so much," says Nona.

"Like my patient, the old lady who wants to die."

"But when you're still 'young,'" says Magda.

"But that's really all we are is leaves on a tree," says Bernadette.

"Animals … I read a book about how old animals die. They go off, they accept it, they understand it, go off into the leaves and lie down and fall asleep."

And the room stops spinning for a moment, it's all black weeping, shredded smoke/fog, slips into NOT for a split moment, no breath, heartbeat, no thought, NO, NOT, NO-THING.

"Some coffee?" asks Magda, Bernadette with her shawl around her skinny shoulders. Nona coughs a small cough and they move out into the kitchen.

## lix.

Magda in her room in the hospital alone, Bernadette "off" getting ready, Nona home with the kids. She'd be there later. Sonia was supposed to come and stay overnight and …

A nurse comes in, syringe in a little white tray.

"What's this for?"

"Relaxant."

Into the right upper arms, sharp almost toothache pain. She waits for it to take effect. It hardly seems to touch her, her massive Slavic nervous system.

She's hungry and thirsty.

"Why can't I even have water beforehand?"

"Because they stick this tube down your throat and there's a strong tendency to vomit and then choke on your own vomit."

Like Glenn Miller … wasn't it Glenn Miller?

Approaching Death, this first small Death … lifetimes of preparation for … dissolving … white salt, black water.

João , the male nurse with the gold teeth, 4,000 Cruceiros a month after twenty years, not even a hundred dollars a month. And at the same time he stays so "nice," his gold-toothed smile so sincere …

Out of the bed on to the hospital cart.

"Nice and relaxed?" asks João.

"Mais ou menos/More or less."

Her body in the skimpy hospital gown, big, but thinner, sleeker, sexier than she could have believed possible – the resurrection of the body. Thanks to Bernadette slowly turning her into a yogic ice-cream sundae.

On her back, down the corridors.

Crucifixes and old yellow-grey shiny paint, Leticia Cavalcanti was saying the other day (a woman she was advising on a dissertation on O'Neill) that she was having a lot of trouble with Lazarus. Laughed, "he laughed because he'd become all-flesh, if the Spirit had triumphed he would have stayed dead."

Into the operating room, the new one.

"Que mais bonito que a outra sala/How much prettier than the other room."

"Não estão mal./Not bad," João smiling.

Bernadette not there yet, another nurse sticking a tube into Magda's left arm, then Bernadette's face hovering over her. How can she look so young, the flesh so tight up under her neck?

Her last surgery, she says. She doesn't care what they think, kisses Magda with an open-mouthed kiss and Magda stirs and secretes "down there."

The anaesthesiologist comes in.

"Tudo bem?/Everything OK?"

"Tudo bem."

""You're sure you don't want to back down?" asks Bernadette.

"Sure."

The tranquillizer working now, swimming in space, psychic dis-/un-membering, her body unremembering itself.

The anaesthesiologist injecting something into the arm-tube now.

"You're going one step further down now."

And slowly it melts into dark and she's there but not there, at the bottom of the Fear Sea, cold, and then beyond … something about waiting for the blood, in case they need it, waiting for the blood, and then out … a long out, a long death, cold, long, the black bottom of the Fearless Sea, and then Bernadette's talking, there's two of them, Bernadette on the left side, another doctor on the right side, and Bernadette's saying she's from Chicago originally but she was married to a Peruvian and can't seem to get rid of the Spanish intonation … and the other doctor answers her Well, the languages are so similar.

Magda can feel them cutting, snipping the flesh, cauterizing, can feel the short electric spurts of pain, then another snip, the catching of the needle into the flesh, pulling it tight.

She tries to talk, Bernadette, I'm awake, I'm getting crucified alive, but she can't talk, can't move her hands or feet, lungs, anything, totally paralysed, a crystal suspended in liquid pain.

She has this terrible sense of being locked up, bound, trapped, wants to get out, tell them she's got to get up, tell them, tell them, tell them, this effort, effort, up on the table in the dark, starts to choke.

"She's pulled the tubes out."

"Vomiting."

And then the hot, long, tortured life-line agony's suddenly all resolved.

## lx.

There wasn't much baggage, really, Magda had been sending boxes up to the states for a long, long time. There was the little box-altar from Minas that she'd put the negroid-featured Virgin and Child (from Bahia) in, the Minas wooden candelabra, the horn and metal candelabra that Beto the Argentinian in the Praça Quince had made so that it ended up looking Mycenaean-Minoan, all the carved boxes and candlesticks from Paraíba and Pernumbuco, the Paraíba "oratorios," you open up a "capsule" and there's Christ in the middle flanked by Peter and Paul, the Amazonian porcupine-quill and fish-scale and seed jewellery ... and her books, of course, the core of her crow-collecting.

The plane left at 6:15 so Bernadette had just stayed overnight, the kids in bed, they'd slept – as always – on Magda's bed under the pineapple-shaped (if you looked carefully) light.

"You blame me in a way, don't you?" asked Bernadette, Nona thinking (Bernadette all in beige, drained out, makeupless, lizardish) how easily she reverted to type, and how more type she became the minute Magda's transforming force was removed. Or would she have reverted back anyhow, was it just a question of time ... ?

"Don't confuse government regulations with feelings," answered Nona, looking at herself in Magda's bedside mirror, asking herself was she drained, drain-ing, reverting too? "If the visa had come through the way we'd dreamed, you'd be coming with us, that's all. And you'll be up there with us within months, months ... "

"I ran into Dr. Queriroz down in the Praça Quinze this morning. I was delivering some more purses to the shoemaker. 'When are you coming back with us?' he asked, like I'd been on vacation ... "

"You're not going back into that!"

"And my father could live another twenty years ... easily ... I mean twenty years with the possibility that every day's the last day. You get that added, extra tension. I could be fifty, fifty-two and still old-man-sitting, and then live on in the same house after he's dead for another forty years alone. He wouldn't have to be there. Sometimes he looks at me like he's dying, not of heart, but dying from not talking. And I blame myself. What does he see through his eyes but a little dry stonewoman, stern, or not even that, dry, dessicated, not stone, salt. He's poised on the edge of the board, all ready to jump, and he looks down and all he sees is just the empty concrete pool ... "

"You're his 'creature,' though, after all ... "

"Sometimes I think all along I've been wrong, that all any of us want is a hug and a few nice words, that that's universal ... the State, the state of THINGS, poverty, maybe they've all shut him up like a closet, and

I used to always blame him for being so closed up, but not any more. Now I blame the world around him. Maybe even myself." Bernadette stops, pours herself and then Nona a little more Vermouth, "It's so empty without Magda isn't it? I've never been so attached to anyone before. I've never been so 'influenced', transformed, like she had this vision of the world ... "

"Inside the star-furnace inside the middle of a purple thistle."

"It's my first murder."

June is the coldest month, everything a suspended, cold, gelatinous green. The roosters, when they do crow, crow muffled under blankets of cold rain. No mosquitos. No one still up Out There. At midnight it feels like three or four or five. Forty degrees. But it feels like forty below.

"Maybe we ought to try to get a little sleep," says Nona.

"OK," says Bernadette, but she means, "can't we talk it out a little," Nona thinking "She's lost her ability to express herself again."

Reverting to type, reverting to silence, beginnings, time runs backwards to where they all began, Nona heavy, unsure, uncertain, frozen, Bernadette afraid, frozen, bitter, shrunken, folded back in on herself. After the ritual of the brushing of the teeth (and pissing) Bernadette goes into 'her' room, Nona goes in with the kids, pulls out the alarm clock, looks at the walls half-expecting, as always, a big black spider spread out across the whiteness ...


#### lxi.

The alarm goes off at 4:15. Nona waking up expecting Magda next to her, finding it hard, for a moment to distinguish between dream and reality. Bernadette's door still closed, the kids sprawled OUT, all hair and camisoles, the medieval Spanish grandeur of the (her) lights, the long corridors, brick walls, the baronial dining-room set, suitcases all packed up against the wall, like a row of stuffed brown dogs. Magda's suitcases. They had to be suede. And she would have liked black, but ...

Nona shivers as she realizes that it's the last time ever that she'll see the blood-lit medievalish Iberian splendour of the dining room, the white diminutiveness of the kitchen, and you walk outside and there's the splendour of the island paradise, with even the expected serpent in the Edenic garden.

She thinks about Sonia. You'd think that Sonia would have been there to say goodbye, would have expected a lineup of ... well, maybe someone'll be at the airport, she thinks, but knows there won't be.

She starts to make herself some fresh coffee, deep dark (raining ... dripping) outside, the dawn (anyhow) never came up like thunder, but trickled its light over the flat, undramatic sky. Will we ever see Bernadette again, really?

The excuse of waiting for an immigrant visa seemed/WAS so lame. She could come up now, punto (period) punto final (final period), and then fight immigration later. As if they'd ever find one solitary illegal immigrant protected under the wings of Mother Patria, Nona herself, who thought of herself as America itself ...

The force gone out of it/them, the debatable, juridical moment of legal-death.

Bernadette's door opens. She's in the kimona she had when she first came into their world, flannel and wing-collared. She was The Nun again.

"Is there time for coffee?"

"Of course. They won't be leaving on time anyhow, with the rain ... "

"And connections?"

"Rio's five hours between planes. You sound like you want to be sure I leave."

Then a sudden upwelling of arms and legs cuddling, explosions of feelings, although ...

Nona asking herself, were they both faking just a little.

Water boiling.

"Let me do this. You can get dressed. The kids ... "

"I do love you, you know that. "

And Nona goes into the big bedroom, pushes, nudges, tugs the girls awake, out of one dream into another. Is she doing the right thing. Such saudade/longing already, remembering the first day at their school Coração de Jesús, the feeling of community, saints and crosses against a cold, blue winter sky ... in Brazil there are no families, but just one big family.

"Come on you guys, we've got to get going."

Alexandra would be the big toughy, the wilful gorgeous one, always on the edge of fat, always on the edge of staying a baby, uncertain, unsure. Margaret would be the big mouth, the hysterical one, thinking, acting, dramatic, always treading water in a circle, always wanting to bring them back down there ...

Full of dreams, visions, hopes ... that it would/could still happen ... that they wouldn't have to leave.

Off with their night things, clothes laid out, a sleep-walk somnambulant ballet.

"Where's Bernadette?" asks Alexandra as she's pulling on her socks.

"She's in the kitchen making coffee."

"She's coming with us?" asks Margaret, pulling on panties, all shivering hair and bones.

"To the airport."

"No, I mean with us."

"Later."

Letting them fend for themselves. She'd like to shower, wash her hair, but …

Pulls on wine-coloured stockings, boots, white bra, wine crêpe blouse with her almost-military wine suede coat. But it's the Armies of Afternoon now, no more Armies of Night …

She expected the plane to be hours late, but when she asked about when it was coming in, she was answered "We're just waiting for it to clear in Camboriú," and they left at seven instead of six-thirty.

"You still blame me, don't you?" Bernadette asking her.

"Don't be silly … "

The kids grabbing on to her. Would Bernadette ever, as she put it, arrumar/arrange a child now?

She would have made such a good mother. Although under all the sexuality she was still such a nun. How could she go back to surgery now?

"O problema se seu./The problem is yours/hers," as Sonia always said.

No one else to see them off. No one. And Brazilian cordiality … ? No more passports to show now, and no overweight, all the months of boxes …

Bernadette's little flower-face in the almost hallucinogenic cold grey dawn, fading, on the bus to the plane, then gone altogether as they took off and circled the island, Nona straining to see Pantanal do Sul, the cemetery where Magda had (jokingly or not?) said she'd like to be buried ("Imagine the romantic pilgrimages to my grave … ") the hot body, hot spirit, now cold facing a cold sea of (almost) perpetual fog.

Couldn't see a thing except mists within mists, clouds, rain, swirling clouds, a glimpse of sea and anonymous island, the beginning or the end of creation, it was hard to say, let's call it the end (here she began to cry) of The Major Phase …